_To Ned_

# TALES
## of the
# ART WORLD

### and other stories

_Much love_
_Philip_

## PHILIP HOOK

MENSCH PUBLISHING

Mensch Publishing
51 Northchurch Road,
London N1 4EE, United Kingdom

First published in Great Britain 2023

A catalogue record for this book is
available from the British Library

ISBN:
978-1-912914-56-2 (paperback)
978-1-912914-57-9 (ebook)

Typeset by Van-garde Imagery, Inc., • van-garde.com

*To Otto, Xander, Ludo, Thea*
*and one to come*

# Contents

# Mrs Ortega's Picasso

Hugo Conrad stared at the painting. An elderly artist with a prodigious erection was depicted in ardent pursuit of a voluptuous female model who, from her expression and pose, appeared not unwilling to pay the ultimate tribute of muse to master. Conrad carefully set his features to convey intelligent concern, aesthetic engagement, and the sort of awe obligatory in front of a work of art by a modern master when the owner of that work is with you in the same room. It was a Picasso, signed and dated 1969. He marvelled at how quickly it seemed to have been executed, at how the paint dripped from the brushstrokes dashed across the white canvas, large expanses of which were left untouched. And he marvelled at the durability of the randy old goat's libido. Picasso must have been 88 when he painted it.

Conrad felt vaguely dislocated, as he often did when parachuted from the relative austerity of his own home life into the drawing rooms of the immensely rich. He was standing here in the hope of persuading the Picasso's owner that Rokeby's was the auction house to sell it for her, and he, as director of its department of Modern Art, was the man to mastermind that operation. Would he succeed? His experience of dealing in high-value art suggested it would be a struggle: generally the more expensive the piece the more difficult its owner. The prospective seller here was an incredibly rich and self-willed woman called Bianca Ortega. He was going to have to turn round in a minute and make some meaningful comment about the picture to her. He caught another glimpse of the artist's erection and his mind went blank.

'Marvellous,' he said.

'Is superb,' agreed Mrs Ortega, lighting another cigarette. How old was she? In her late seventies, he guessed. But it was difficult to tell. Her body was a work of restoration in progress: certain sections of her face were unnaturally taut, as if cling-film had been stretched over her cheek and jaw bones, while her lips were swollen in a caricature of amplitude and set to a default position expressive of ill-natured surprise. But what Hugo particularly wondered at, as something of a connoisseur of the ambitious cosmetic reconstruction work undertaken by the more intrepid of his rich clientele, was the condition of her breasts, inflated to a geometric perfection and artfully exposed by a low-cut T-shirt worn under her dark blue Lanvin jacket. They were a triumph.

He reflected that those breasts symbolised something momentous, could indeed in certain respects be seen as linchpins of the entire western capitalist system. Mrs Ortega, a woman rich enough to buy great art, deployed some of her wealth on the quest for youth that the alchemy of cosmetic surgery promised; the cosmetic surgeons purveying this service grew so rich that they too started buying expensive paintings. Hugo had noticed an increasing number of them competing in Rokeby's auctions. Here was a perfect illustration of the drip-down effect of wealth operating to the economic benefit of society. Or of cosmetic surgeons, anyway. And, tangentially, of art dealers and auction houses.

In the end, Conrad reflected, the world in which he operated could be divided into two groups: a relatively small one comprising the already fabulously rich, and a rather larger one comprising those who by providing services to the fabulously rich aspired to become fabulously rich themselves. A dance ensued between the service-consumers and the service-providers. Just occasionally one of the aspirants would succeed spectacularly enough to cross the line from provider to consumer. Or, more dangerously, they would be so seduced by exposure to the trappings of wealth that they started living like their clients, without having amassed sufficient wherewithal to carry it off. A shortcut to success was for a service-provider to marry a fabulously rich person. Hugo inspected Madame Ortega covertly. No. There were limits to professional ambition.

A butler came in with a tray of coffee and some chic little biscuits, which you were meant to take from the proffered plate with one of the tiny linen napkins edged in lace that were simultaneously held out for you. Hugo took one, and a little napkin. People were forever coming in and out of the cavernous white drawing room where Mrs Ortega had received him; a lawyer just now, with something for her to sign; a secretary before that, with an invitation for her acceptance or refusal; and a man in a white coat, five minutes earlier, whose presence was unexplained. Could he perhaps have been some sort of physician, on emergency standby with a syringe of Botox?

What the situation called for, Hugo felt, was a further expression of his aesthetic engagement with the painting in front of him. He dredged deep into his repertoire of suitable gambits and came up with a trusty quotation from Balzac. It was to the effect that those whose passion is for works of art are fortunate, for the objects of their affections never grow old. He stopped himself in time. Anything to do with the ageing process was best avoided with someone as close to her cosmetic surgeon as Mrs Ortega. No. If in doubt, say something about the subject of the work. 'Artist and model,' he murmured vaguely.

'*Que?*'

'Artist and model. One of the great subjects. It has a time-less quality.'

'Is Rumpy-Pumpy.'

'Ah. Yes.'

'You know I met him once.'

'Who?'

'Picasso. In Nice, in 1970. I was very young woman.'

'How fascinating. What was he like?'

'He was sex maniac. With garlic breath.'

Hugo laughed politely. 'He had a number of muses, didn't he?' he said. He meant it as a joke, but it came out rather primly.

'Muses, Mr Conrad? What is muses?'

'Models. Women who inspired him. Artistically, I mean.'

'Ah! Many, many women. *Si*. Is natural, he was artist. Was good he lived before Internet Dating, huh? Otherwise there would have been too many – how you say? – 'muses'.' She cackled throatily at the thought of Picasso's indiscriminate pursuit of the opposite sex. He may have been a very old man; but, as Mrs Ortega implied, that wasn't the point. He was an artist. That conjured unconventional responses from womankind, particularly if musehood was on offer. But not from Mrs Ortega, it seemed.

'Of course mine is one of the best of the late works,' she went on. 'So I am always told. By experts.' She emphasised the last word as if to indicate that she wasn't yet convinced by Hugo's own claim to be categorised within their number, a claim that would only be validated by his agreement that the painting before him was indeed amongst the most important of the artist's final years. Was it? The answer was sadly not. It was a little above average, no more.

In fact Conrad had private reservations about late works by Picasso. A lot of them were very cursorily executed; some were actually pretty bad. There had once been a school of critical thought which acknowledged that a proportion of what the master produced post 1960 was evidence of either his senility or his cynical mockery of an art world that lapped them up so voraciously. That was before late Picasso was discovered by Contemporary Art collectors: once the aesthetics of Contemporary Art were drawn into the equation, all late Picasso became indiscriminately sought after. Someone noticed the resemblance of late Picasso to the work of Jean-Michel Basquiat. Basquiat (black, gay, died young) was an artist of such desirability that his name could only be uttered in a hoarse whisper by Contemporary Art collectors. Picasso's late work was conclusively sanctified by the association.

Hugo recognised that these were not thoughts to share with Mrs Ortega. At least her example was painted in striking co-lours. It was reasonably large, looked highly recognisable as a Picasso, and best of all boasted a very prominent signature. But Hugo was conscious of the need to preserve a delicate balance in his response to the painting he was now confronting. Yes, he must get across that he yielded to no-one in his understand-ing and appreciation of this phase of Picasso's *oeuvre*. But he didn't want to give Mrs Ortega too much encouragement. If he praised her example too lavishly, she would undoubtedly up her asking price.

'It's fascinating art-historically,' he ventured.

She frowned at him. This was not good enough. Unnerved, he added recklessly, 'And of course it's a very striking work. Iconic.'

She nodded, appeased. Iconic. He had over-compensated. But then again, everything in the art world was now iconic. As a purveyor of great art, you risked credibility by offering to the market anything that could not be described as iconic. He hur-ried on, 'When did you acquire it?'

'My second husband, he bought it from that gallery in Switzerland. I do not remember the name, but it must have been in the late 1970s. I was very young woman then. It was a gift for me. He was a generous man, Gottardo. He totally adored me, of course.'

Hugo could not recall precisely how many husbands she had run through. At least three, he thought. She was without one at the moment, but from very early on in life she had demonstrated that rare knack perfected by a very few fortunate women of only marrying extremely rich men. Did such things happen by accident or design? It was easy to typecast these egregious cases of serial matrimony and inheritance as the product of remorseless gold-digging, but perhaps there was more to it than that. Perhaps it was a matter of chemistry; perhaps every so often an exceptional woman was born who gave off something hormonal that irresistibly attracted men with money. If so, bottling it for redistribution would be a worthwhile project. Whatever the explanation, each of Mrs Ortega's husbands had left her fabulously well provided for, particularly the last whose demise five years ago had meant she was now in control of one of Europe's largest industrial conglomerates. She hadn't done badly for a girl from murky and never quite clarified Eastern European origins.

Hugo paused to consider how to play it. He had been invited here because Mrs Ortega wanted to sell this picture. He must make it easy for her. 'It's fascinating how the greatest art collections, and the greatest art collectors, are constantly evolving,' he told her. 'You can enjoy a work for a number of years and then feel it's the right moment to move on from it to something else. And the marvellous thing is that your selling it allows someone else the pleasure of its ownership. You're committing an act of sharing.'

'An act of sharing'. Had he really said that? Dear God. But at least he was warming up now, getting the words out with more fluency. She contemplated Hugo doubtfully. Then she shook her head with an expression of saintly suffering nobly borne. 'Always possessions, possessions. I think to sell. I want less possessions in my life.'

'I understand. You want to live more... more simply.'

'No! No! No! Mr Conrad. Never more simply. Always big parties, flowers, the best champagne, everything perfect.'

'Of course... I didn't mean to suggest...'

'Do you know how big is this house? It has largest ballroom in the city. I cannot even count the bedrooms. Why should I count the bedrooms? I have better things to do. I am business-woman... head of an empire. See this magazine?' She seized a glossy periodical and waved it in Hugo's direction. 'It is business magazine, serious financial journal. And who do they interview? They interview me.'

'Of course they do, Mrs Ortega.'

'Not *Hello* magazine. Never *Hello* magazine.'

'No, you're quite right to have nothing to do with them.'

'They beat my door down, these people,' she went on. 'They want big feature, every month. They know no-one gives parties like my parties. But I say no. No, no, no.'

A wild look had entered her eye. Things were threatening to get out of hand. Hugo must calm her down. 'Obviously I would handle the sale of your Picasso with utmost discretion. It would be a private transaction, no-one would know you were selling. I would ensure total anonymity for you.'

'Si, of course.' She seemed mollified. 'Is essential, the confidentiality.' Hugo realised this was significant. It was also significant that she hadn't come up with the cry that rich owners often afflicted him with, just as he seemed to be convincing them of the desirability of achieving a sale: 'Yes, but what would I do with the money?' That was what made him want to beat them round the head with a rolled-up newspaper. Or a croquet mallet.

But Bianca Ortega hadn't voiced the question about what to do with the proceeds of the sale of her Picasso. Therefore she needed the cash. Her business empire perhaps wasn't quite as successful as she made out. The European economy was still sluggish of course. And the laundry costs for her little napkins couldn't be negligible, either. Could it be that she was that glorious phenomenon 'a motivated seller'? In that case she would need the transaction to be kept as secret as possible, to avoid the erosion of confidence in her businesses that any publicity about her selling expensive art would precipitate. Hugo set his own features into an expression of rigorous discretion, that of a man who took his secrets with him to the grave.

'You can have total trust in me, Mrs Ortega. Only three people in the world will know about this transaction: you, me and the buyer.'

She nodded thoughtfully. 'So what do you think it's worth?'

'I think I know someone who would pay $15 million for it.'

'You are joking, of course. I do not sell for less than $25 million.'

'Ah. Well.' He must think quickly. Was it worth $25 million? What was anything worth in this rapidly accelerating market? 'A similar one made $15 million last year.'

She was ready for him. 'Yes, but that was last year. And mine is better. Mine is larger.'

He turned back to look at the work of art itself, and peered at it intensely.

'Perhaps I could ask 20,' he conceded, still staring at the picture. 'I have a very good client in mind for it... perhaps they could be persuaded to pay a premium for such an important work. And of course it hasn't been on the market for many years. And I don't think you've ever lent it for exhibition, have you. It's got a wonderful freshness. Yes, if you were prepared to give me exclusivity for three months, I would take it on at 20. Definitely. Shall we proceed on that basis?'

He turned round. She wasn't there anymore. He was talking to an empty room. Ah. He found himself pacing up and down with a benign, somewhat vacant smile on his face. The door opened and the butler re-entered, this time carrying a tray of little pieces of rye bread dressed with caviar. Hugo took one. And a little napkin. The butler nodded, then disappeared.

To pass the time, Hugo inspected the silver-framed photographs spread promiscuously over a large tabletop in a corner of the room. Here they were, the continental plutocracy: people at parties, people on boats, people skiing. Frenchmen in dinner jackets and dark glasses. Italians with impossibly sleek silver hair. Bronzed Germans smiling wolfishly from expensive sports cars. These were men who wore corduroy trousers ironed to an impeccable crease, dangerously effeminate shoes, and frequently went without socks. Some even clicked heels and affected to kiss the hands of the opposite sex when introduced to them. These were women who dressed stylishly and expensively and did not, like their dowdier English counterparts, give the impression they would rather be grooming horses or breeding dogs. These were people the lines on whose faces were the product, in the words of Nancy Mitford, not of thought but of sun. In one photograph Hugo saw Frank Sinatra with someone whom it was just possible to identify as a much younger Bianca Ortega. In another, somewhat incongruously, there was a veiled and suitably reverent Bianca Ortega receiving a personal blessing from His Holiness the Pope.

From a distant quarter of the house he now heard voices raised in acrimonious argument. One of them was his hostess's. The second was that of an unidentified woman. A door slammed. There was silence again.

A minute later Mrs Ortega came back into the room. She looked mutinous but regal. 'My daughter, she is crazy woman,' she said. 'She has lost her reason.'

'I'm... I'm sorry to hear it.'

'You know how many pairs of shoes she has?'

'Um... no.'

'Tell me. How many you think?'

Estimates, estimates. His expertise was constantly being put to the test. 'Um. Twenty?'

Madame Ortega gave a little sigh of disdain at the feebleness of his calculatory powers. 'Four hundred and fifty pairs.'

'God. That's certainly... certainly a lot.'

'My daughter, she wishes to travel this afternoon with four hundred and fifty pairs. She is sick. We must take a larger plane to Marbella just to fit in her shoes.'

'Ah. Yes. That's... er.... difficult. I do see.' Hugo saw many things. He saw that the encumbrance of four hundred and fifty pairs of shoes would present a logistical nightmare. He saw that being rich brings with it unimagined challenges. He saw that being Mrs Ortega's daughter might not be easy, either.

'So. I am busy woman. Thank you, Mr Conrad, that you came to visit me.'

'And the Picasso?'

'I sell it through you, but for $24 million. Net. To me. You have eight weeks exclusive. Make the contract with my lawyers.'

Hugo caught the afternoon flight back to London. He settled comfortably into his window seat and accepted a glass of champagne from the pretty stewardess. It hadn't been a bad morning's work. Who was to say that Rokeby's couldn't get $27 million for Mrs Ortega's painting, to include ten per cent for the auction house? These were exciting times for the art market. All you were really selling was fantasy, anyway, fantasy garnished with social aspiration. The charming stewardess topped him up with more champagne, and he felt his cares melting away. Yes, $27 million was eminently achievable.

As the plane began its descent into Heathrow, he allowed himself a celebratory third glass. A Picasso was a Picasso, after all.

# Angel Hut

Ed Rowley looked at himself in the bathroom mirror and felt depressed. So old, so dispiritingly old. Eyes puffy. Cheeks sagging. Hair thinning. Torso thickening. Man-breasts drooping, paunch spreading. God, to be thirty years younger. To be agile again. To get out of bed in the morning with no joints aching. To stride on to the cricket field in the full glory of his prime. White on green. The clink of plates in the pavilion carrying across the grass to the wicket. For some, heaven might be eating *foie gras* to the sound of trumpets. Not for him. No, the greatest pleasure that life could offer was the perfectly timed cover drive, unerringly struck smack in the middle of the bat. Only one thing to rival it, and that was the triumph of taking a really sharp catch in the slips. That instant reaction. Something beyond mind-eye co-ordination, a matter not of science but of instinct. But an instinct that had gradually lost its potency. A bit like the libido, a poor largely dormant thing now, only occasionally stirred into brief episodes of wistful lust by the chance glimpse of an unattainable young woman's neck or breast, the curve of her buttock or the line of her thigh. When you had a body as old and flabby as his had grown, the key to sexual continence was no more than a functioning sense of the ridiculous.

That last game of cricket, five years ago: it was still something he returned to as a marker of irrevocable decline, as a nadir of personal inadequacy. He had scratched around the crease for twenty minutes in scoring three edgy and maladroit runs before spooning up a catch to mid-off. Much better to be out first ball than to offer such extended evidence of waning powers. It had come at the end of a season in which he had not reached double figures in any of his five innings. Although he affected nonchalance about averages, he was a secret assembler of statistics. Particularly his own. In one glorious year in his prime he had amassed 1,156 runs at an average of 68. The grim product of that last season, by contrast, had been an aggregate of 23 and an average of just under 6. He was embarrassing himself. But almost worse was what happened when he fielded that day. He stood corpulently defiant at first slip and managed to spill three chances in a row, two of them pretty straightforward. Patrick had put an arm round his shoulder after the third and told him bad luck, old cock. They either stick or they don't. But other teammates, beyond earshot in the outfield, were no doubt less generous about his diminishing performance. A passenger, that was what he had become. Those three dropped catches were ingrained in his memory. He still relived each one in vivid detail, that sense of empty horror as the ball ended up not in the practised safety of his hands but rolling away mockingly and subversively on the turf. After that game he had called it a day. He'd lost it. And he didn't want to go on advertising the fact.

The first year after he'd given up cricket had been a strange one. It was as if turning his back on the game had set in motion a chain reaction of redefinitions in his life. One of the first things he did that winter was split up with Daphne. It was surprisingly easy, what they call an amicable separation. She'd gone back to live in Gloucestershire. She was happiest there, with the garden. The children were adults now, living their own lives, and he was freed up to live his own. So he'd taken early retirement. He kept the flat in London, based himself there. Went to Lord's quite a lot in summer. Played some bridge in winter. Maybe he was drinking a bit more, but what the hell? What was he saving himself for, anyway? But just occasionally, when he inspected himself in the bathroom mirror, he thought about them again. The halcyon days.

Mind you, this was some bathroom mirror. The light flooded in through the window. Full, glorious sunlight, warming the tiles beneath his feet. The sky an azure blue. He could hear the waves breaking on the beach. He'd left behind the bloody British winter. February in London, cooped up in a mansion flat, was no joke. That was when fourth floor lateral life became claustrophobic, when the first gin and tonic was broached earlier and earlier in the day, when he settled down to afternoon movies that he never saw the end of because as darkness fell around 4.30 he would be gently snoring on the sofa. So when Patrick invited him to spend two weeks in Florida that month he accepted gratefully. Couple of bachelors, Patrick said. Get up to some mischief. He was now in a routine of swimming in the sea every day. There was a lot of lounging in the sun, and a lot of eating and drinking. In fact it was pretty bloody marvellous. Patrick had got it right, selling up his business and buying an apartment here. Lucky bastard. But he was a good man, Patrick. And a good mate.

'Want a nightcap?' suggested Patrick that evening. They were driving back to Palm Beach after dinner, through that hinterland of bungaloid nail-parlours, topless bars, and evangelical churches which is coastal Florida. It was a warm velvet night. If it hadn't been for the ceaseless passage of automobiles along the highway, you could have heard the bullfrogs singing.

Patrick knew his way about. He pulled into the parking lot of a neon-lit place called 'The Angel Hut'. As they went in, a black man with an eye-patch demanded their ID.

'I'm afraid I've left my passport back in the house,' Ed said to Patrick.

'Just show them anything.'

He offered his MCC Membership card. The one-eyed black man peered at it, shrugged, and handed it back to him. They were allowed inside.

They sat at the bar and drank beer. A couple of bored-looking pole-dancers – presumably the angels whose hut this was – gyrated on a stage. They were almost the only customers in the place.

'Either of these two lovelies get you going?' inquired Patrick.

Their skins were smooth and their bodies were curvaceous enough. They undulated in the right places. But they did nothing for him. Perhaps it was the resolute way they chewed gum as they danced. Ed stared at them willing himself to feel something, but it was like trying to strike a match in a force ten gale. Their flesh carried no more of an erotic charge than a drawing in a medical text book. Or a carcase in an abbatoir.

'Probably not, no. What about you?'

'Resistible. Very resistible.'

They were preparing to move on when the pony-tailed barman told them that the show was about to start.

'What show?' they asked.

'Britney's show.' The two pole dancers spat out their gum and shuffled off to their dressing rooms. They were replaced on stage by another girl. Blond, tall, with powerful thighs. A shade overweight. But striking, somehow. There was an air of aggressive defiance about her.

'What does Britney do?'

'What doesn't she do. Ain't no-one like Britney this side of Fort Lauderdale.'

The barman ushered them forward into a position closer to the stage, where they stood in self-conscious anticipation. Britney stepped out of the only clothing she was wearing, a brief thong, and stood facing away from them. A box of golf balls was placed on a small table next to her. The music stepped up its tempo.

Britney took a golf ball from the box, inserted it into her private parts, then leant forward with her legs apart, grasping the pole for support. Her buttocks moved in time with the music. Suddenly a small, hard, white, spherical object shot between Patrick and himself at tremendous speed.

'Jesus!' said Patrick. 'That could have taken my eye out.'

Ed wondered about the doorman's eye-patch.

'Imagine the muscles she must have to generate speed like that,' mused Patrick.

Britney was not finished yet. She was inserting another golf ball. Involuntarily, Patrick and he crouched next to each other. He was in the position he had vowed never to adopt again. He was fielding in the slips.

Two more golf balls cannoned between them at high speed. Ed only registered their trajectory sometime after they had passed and bounced into the darker area of the room behind them. The second ball sounded as though it had broken a glass. Suddenly, irrationally he became gripped with the idea of actually catching one of these missiles. Insanity, of course. Even Ben Stokes in his prime would have been challenged to get his hands anywhere near.

But in sport, just occasionally, you do something in the heat of the moment of which you didn't know you were capable. The fourth ball flew off at an unexpected angle to his right. He shot out his hand. And it stuck. It was the sort of reaction he thought he would never experience again: intuitive, unthinking, sublime. You don't realise you've done it till afterwards. And this time it unleashed a forgotten emotion. He felt an unfamiliar surge of pure elation. An elation that took him back thirty years.

'Still got it, haven't you, you old bastard,' said Patrick as he opened the car door in the parking lot. 'That was some catch.'

'She's some girl,' he murmured.

'Who, Britney?'

'I think I'm in love.'

'It would be like going to bed with a bowling machine. You'd have to pad up and wear a helmet.'

They laughed. They laughed themselves sick.

But when he got back to London, he still had the golf-ball. He put it in his desk. Once or twice a month he would take it out and rub it between the palms of his hands, even toss it in the air and catch it a few times before replacing it reverently in the drawer.

# War Artist

## Flanders, 1917

'Are they maps th'art drawing, sir? Is that what th'art doing?'

'Yes, Arkwright, you could call them that. They're kind of maps, in a manner of speaking.'

'Maps of enemy positions, like, is that what they are?'

Arkwright was a strong young man, a coal miner in civilian life. His broad, bronzed brow was furrowed in the effort to understand, to give me the benefit of the doubt. Because there was a doubt in his mind, an unspoken question: what was I actually doing here on the front line, an officer with the rank of captain, an officer as whose batman Arkwright was serving, what was I doing living in the mess with the other officers, armed with a rifle and a hand gun and several rounds of ammunition, drinking their whisky and eating their sausages and their Gentleman's Relish, but when the whistles blew and the Very lights flared and the rattles crackled, where was I? Why was I not going over the top into the carnage at the head of a platoon of troops like my brother officers? What was this strange, apparently privileged existence that I led? I was of it, but not in it. Holding back, being held back. Why?

So that I could make these drawings, drawings that Arkwright had decided to construe as maps. Because as maps, these drawings of mine meant something, justified me, and by extension justified Arkwright himself. If what I was creating on these pieces of paper could be validated as playing some crucial role in the military effort that we were all part of, if my drawings were offering carefully assessed and cleverly calculated routes forward to enemy lines, if they were instruments of surprise, documents of superior military know-how, then it all made sense. I was doing something that would guide us to victory quicker and reduce our casualties. Thanks to my maps we could surprise them, those filthy Hun, drive them back to where they came from, shut them up forever. And protect the lives of Arkwright and his comrades, the lads he'd volunteered with in Barnsley, trained with in Catterick and in whose company he had been shipped over the sea to Northern France for the great adventure, a first and thrilling glimpse of a world beyond Yorkshire. Except that no-one had told him that this great continental tour he'd been inspired into undertaking was a parody of foreign travel, that he and his mates had mostly only been issued with one-way tickets.

Of course by this point in the war Arkwright needed no reminding of the horror that his first jaunt overseas had developed into. Large numbers of his fellow Barnsley boys would indeed never return to Yorkshire. They were now deconstructed into body parts and scattered at strange angles over the landscape of northern France: dismembered legs and arms arranged in abstract compositions across barbed wire, single fingers fought over by the rats of no-man's land, a human ear floating in the rainwater of a shell hole.

Whistling tunelessly, Arkwright gathered up my boots and took them away for cleaning. I was left sitting in my socks in the Mess with my drawings on my knee in front of me, trying to see them through Arkwright's eyes. Perhaps they did look like maps, these landscapes of the battlefield that I had interpreted in constantly shifting angles lit by strange and unexpected contrasts of light and dark, patterns of flare and shadow, unearthly, hellish, contorted, punctuated by stunted trees, twisted into caricatures of natural growth. What did Arkwright think when he saw those trees? I sensed that he couldn't afford to interpret them in the way that I did, as icons of destruction and despair. No, for Arkwright they had to be diagrammatic symbols, markers of military significance in an expanse otherwise bereft of distinguishing features, necessary signposts on a route forward to victory.

And when they went back to London, these carefully packed sheets of paper bearing my signs and symbols and marks, and when they were framed and glazed and hung on some plush gallery wall in the vicinity of elegant Bond Street, what would be their purpose then? To tell the truth about what men like Arkwright and his comrades were going through on that front line? To open the eyes of comfortable civilian England to the reality of trench warfare? No, not the truth. A lyricised version of it; or, in my case, a cubicised version of it. It made me uneasy.

Here I was exploiting the sufferings of these Barnsley infantry-men as the raw material for my own artistic expression. I was pitting my daring as a modernist against their daring as soldiers. Whose audacity was the more courageous? Not mine, I feared. It was the verdict Arkwright would have reached, too, had he been in full possession of the facts. A map to Arkwright would have military value. A drawing of a battlefield, on the other hand, would have struck him as superfluous, insultingly and inexplicably self-indulgent.

There had been kind friends who had assured me that what I was doing was important, very important. You're like a war correspondent, they said, a journalist on the front line, except your despatches are even more worthwhile because they're works of visual art. How else are the people at home going to be kept informed of what's really going on? How are they going to understand? And then there had been Gubbins. Gubbins was a rebel, a socialist, a man who didn't compromise. 'You're going to be a war artist?' he exclaimed in disbelief. 'So you've capitulated, have you? Joined the propaganda department. Because that's all you'll be producing, I can promise you that. Reassuring pap for the masses. Patriotism packaged for the man on the Clapham Omnibus. I don't care if you're a Cubist: you're prostituting your art to shore up a shameful war.'

'So you think I shouldn't be going out there to the front line?' I challenged Gubbins.

'I think you should only go out there if you're prepared to make a statement.'

'What kind of statement?'

24

'Hoist a white flag, walk over to the German trenches, and seek out your enemy equivalent, the German war artist.'

'Really, Gubbins? What should I do then?'

'First you should shake him by the hand. Then you should both shoot each other.'

Ten minutes later Arkwright was back with my boots. They were shining clean, a work of art really. A pity I was very shortly going to have to soil them once more in the slush and sewage that swilled around in the bottom of the trenches. Somewhere in that morass lay duckboards that had long since sunk into the mud.

'Thank you, Arkwright,' I said in dismissal. But he stood there, uncharacteristically indecisive. There was something else on his mind, beyond his uncertainty about what I was actually drawing on those sheets of paper of mine.

''Ast tha got moment, sir?'

'What is it, Arkwright?'

'Ah need soom advice, like.'

'I'll help if I can. What's it about?'

'It's Private Entwistle, sir. 'E's not right in 'is 'ead. The lad needs help.'

'We all have moments when we feel a bit down,' I said feebly.

'Nay, it's not like that. 'E were allus the strong one. 'E and Ah grew up together in Barnsley. I've known 'im all my life, boy and man. Nowt daunted 'im like. Now 'e won't 'ardly speak, and if 'e do, 'e don't make no sense.'

'It sounds like…' I'd been going to say shell shock, but suddenly remembered the instructions we were under from higher up. No-one was to mention those two words. They were eradicated from the language of the army. They didn't exist. They were a dangerous concept, bad for morale. So I said, 'Has he seen the MO?'

'MO says there's nowt wrong with him. Says 'e's malingering, like. But Ah know different. Bob Entwistle's no more malingerer than Ah am. Summat's snapped in lad's head.'

'What about the Padre? Has he spoken to the Padre, maybe he can help?'

Arkwright sighed and shook his head hopelessly. 'Padre's just going to tell him to go on fighting good fight on God's behalf. That won't cut no ice with Bob Entwistle, not any more. Ahm that worried abaht poor boogger. He's not hissell, like. He might do summat daft.'

One thing I knew about soldiers like Arkwright: their loyalty was to their country, to their regiment, to their commanding officer, in variable order of priority. But their greatest loyalty, which trumped all the rest, was to their immediate fellow-soldiers, to their mates. It was what drove them over the top into enemy fire, it was what compelled them into actions of extraordinary valour. They mustn't let their mates down. If that obligation broke, the perceived necessity to look out for your comrade, then woe betide the British army. Or any army, come to that.

That night there was a big push. Wave after wave of infantry went forward from our trenches. I drank several whiskies and took up position in the casualty station to make drawings of the cease-less traffic in mortality that surged through the tents on nights like this. In our small intensely-disputed section of the line it was by now a matter of simple mathematics: for every ten yards gained, the going rate was one hundred lives. A hundred outward tickets that needed no returns. Around 1 a.m. they brought Arkwright in. He had lost an arm and a foot and half his face, so I felt a kind of relief when a few minutes later an orderly told me he had just died. I drew him, a quick sketch of his mangled body as it lay on the stretcher. Would this sketch help the war effort? Would Arkwright, if he awoke briefly from the dead and ran his eye over it, still be able to interpret it as an important piece of military intelligence, like a map or a diagram, that would be of value to our troops and help bring victory nearer? Or would it just end up as one more exhibit at that plush Mayfair Gallery, a composition for people to nod critically over before going on to lunch in the Ritz? 'Yes, I can see it's a dead soldier, but why are the angles all haywire? They'll never persuade me, those Cubists, that they know what they're do-ing. It's just laziness, because they can't draw properly.'

The same night that Arkwright died, Private Entwistle de-serted. As their unit went over the top together into the murder-ous machine-gun fire that fatally damaged Arkwright, Entwistle ran away. Instead of pulling himself over the sandbags and running forward with the lads, he clambered out of the back of the trench and staggered off in the opposite direction. He disappeared into the distance, towards our own artillery em-placements, through the relentless shelling of the enemy guns. Unfortunately he wasn't hit. Military Police found him the following afternoon, sitting in the shade of an elm next to a deserted farm building a mile and a half back. He had located one of the very few trees that still had its branches intact and even a covering of leaves. It was decided to make an example of him. He was court-martialled forty-eight hours later and sentenced to death by firing squad.

I felt I should do something for Entwistle, if only out of respect for the memory of Arkwright. Entwistle was in the care of the padre for his last night on earth. He was due to be executed at dawn. I offered to sit with the prisoner for half an hour, so the padre could go and get something to eat.

'I am afraid he's not saying very much,' the padre told me.

'Understandable, I suppose.' I had brought my sketch book with me. 'Would he mind if I made a quick drawing of him, do you think?'

'Can't do any harm. It might help take his mind off things, poor fellow.'

It was a Cubist portrait. I called it 'Soldier Crying', all jagged angles and displaced lips and cheekbones and what may or may not have been tear drops in the crevices between the compressions of form and space. Yes, if Arkwright had seen it and held it upside down he might just have persuaded himself that it was a map of military terrain.

But no, I don't think I sent that one back to the Gallery for the exhibition.

# Galactico

Oleg woke up nervous that Saturday. He could barely eat breakfast. There was a sick feeling of apprehension laced with anticipation in his stomach. It was a familiar feeling, and it only grew stronger as the morning progressed. The apprehension he could cope with, just about. What was much more dangerous was the anticipation. That was the emotion to beware of.

'So you are going to your football game this afternoon?' said his wife Ivana when he met her in the drawing room. Their lives did not intersect much, although they lived in the same houses, sometimes even in the same one at the same time.

'Of course. You are coming with me?' He sincerely hoped she wasn't. There were some activities in his life where he could tolerate her company. Football was not one of them.

She shook her head, pausing to adjust her mascara in a mirror. 'Uh, uh. There is shopping I must do.'

'So. I will see you this evening maybe.'

She turned away from the mirror and looked at him. She was wearing a leather jacket and leather boots. She was still a good-looking woman, he reflected with a kind of idle interest. Now she said, 'You look terrible, Oleg. You look eaten up inside.'

He shrugged. 'I have things to think about. Business matters.'

'You are foolish man, you know that, Oleg?'

'What do you mean?'

'Why do you allow your happiness to be dictated by eleven young men who you barely know kicking a ball round a football field? What are these young men to you? These young men are Nothing.'

They had had this conversation before. 'Look,' he told her, 'they may be eleven young men that I barely know as human beings, but I know them as footballers. They are mine. I have bought them and sold them and they are my creation, OK? Once they are out on that pitch, I care about them. I am sorry. That's the way I'm made.'

'You know what you want to get yourself? A good shrink.'

Maybe she was right, reflected Oleg. She often was. Which didn't make her opinion any more acceptable.


Oleg's driver was ready for him at 1 p.m. Oleg slid into the back seat and as they eased out of the electric gates he was comforted to note the immediate presence of the two security cars that always accompanied him on any journey into the outside world, one in front and one behind. He settled down to check his emails: there was an oil deal to approve, and the sale of some real estate in Moscow. And the big steel deal seemed to be going through, after six months of protracted negotiations. But he couldn't really focus. As they got closer to the stadium he was aware of increasing numbers of supporters wearing the familiar red and white scarves and hats and replica shirts thronging the streets. They clustered in large numbers outside cafes and bars, milling about, drinking, shouting, gesticulating into telephones, moving with a sort of restless purpose, a suppressed belligerence. The atmosphere of expectation was almost tangible. He was protected from recognition by the black glass. One hour forty minutes until kick-off, he noted, as the car was waved swiftly through three security barriers and drew up at the main entrance. He got out quickly and hurried inside, but not before he had been cheered by a group of by-standing fans. 'Good luck, Oleg mate!' they called after him. They loved him, as well they should. He had brought them undreamed of success and happiness. Until he had taken over their club they had been a turgidly lower mid-table team, never winning anything, occasionally even being relegated. In the past five years they had won six trophies. He was not far off from a divinity to these people.

He was ushered swiftly up in the elevator to his private office, just off the main directors' box. Katinka was there waiting for him, brisk, efficient, smiling, impenetrable. Katinka was Anoushka's assistant. That made her his secretary's secretary. Katinka herself had an assistant, Olga, his secretary's secretary's secretary. All three of them were cast in the same mould: brisk, efficient, smiling, unemotional. He did not want emotion from the people who worked for him. He had quite enough of that to cope with in his private life. He just wanted things done, efficiently. His cars to be ready for him, his helicopters hovering, his jets prepared for take-off the moment he stepped into them from the just-landed helicopter. Now he needed to be alone for a while. 'No visitors, Katinka. And no calls, OK?' He needed to be protected from the myriad hangers-on, would-be business associates and well-wishers who were already lining up to shake his hand or greet him with unctuous platitudes. 'No problem, Oleg.' She withdrew discreetly, shutting the door behind her. He sighed and sat down. It was early in the day, but his nerve needed steadying. He reached for the vodka bottle and poured himself a shot. Let us win today. We have to win today. Let us not fail to win today.

When Oleg bought the football club he thought it was just another possession, like the jet or the houses or the yachts or the energy companies or the wife or the girlfriends that he already owned and controlled. But it turned out not to be. It turned out to be oddly and infuriatingly unreliable. He stuffed the team with expensive players, bought the very best in the world, Brazilians, Spaniards, Dutchmen, even an Englishman (though he was threatening to be one of his more expensive mistakes) and he hired a manager with an unrivalled record of success. And yet though his team won most of their matches they still sometimes lost. It was baffling and upsetting. Those defeats – and draws, too, sometimes - kept him awake at night in a way that none of his other concerns did. It was the one area of his life which would not submit to his total control, the one area where he suffered the unfamiliar emotion of frustration. For that reason it fascinated him. He couldn't stop thinking about it. He went through phases of firing his coaches and replacing them.

But while they all won a lot of games for him, it was rare that one coach was conspicuously more successful than another. The football pitch was the one field of activity in which his wealth did not automatically ensure that he always got what he wanted. That failure to win gave him pain in a way that almost everything else irksome didn't, cushioned as it was by his wealth. Ivana had said he was a fool to allow his happiness to be dictated by eleven young men he barely knew kicking a ball round a football field. He had told her that he *did* know them, he knew them as footballers, that because he had bought them and sold them they were his creation. He might have added that, while he did not really know them as human beings, their very names had become components of his happiness. When he thought about them, those names gave him pleasure or pain, depending on their most recent performances on the pitch. In a way he was in love with them. Not with their physical bodies, but with what they symbolised, with the moments they had made him happy with their goals or sad with their defeats.

And something else, something deeply dispiriting. He recognised in himself that he was growing more downcast by the occasional failure of his team to win than he was uplifted by their regular victories. How could this be happening? He remembered the sheer joy of the occasion, in the second year of his ownership of the club, when they had won the national championship for the first time. This is perfection, he told himself. This is the peak of my life's happiness. This must happen again. But when it did, it was less enthralling. And the third time they achieved it, there was even an element of anticlimax.

Success was in a strange way disappointing. But then last season they failed to win the title, finishing second, and Oleg felt suicidal. Oh, God. The disappointment of failing to win was even worse than the disappointment of winning. Perhaps Ivana was right about the shrink.

About half an hour before the game started he went back into the main directors' box and shook a few people's hands. He spoke briefly on the mobile to the manager, down in the dressing room. 'Guillermo not starting today?' 'No,' said Franz cautiously. 'The plan is to bring him on after 60 minutes. If we need him.' 'You're the boss.' Oleg always said that to all his managers, although of course it wasn't strictly true. Then he went out and watched the stadium filling. Very soon there would be 50,000 people in the ground. 47,000 of them would be passionately committed to the home side. To his side. Sometimes the sense of yearning that emanated from those 47,000 throats simultaneously was almost unbearable. It was the yearning for victory, yearning for that one extra goal that would carry the day. The noise they made was thrilling and poignant and powerful. And it expressed everything he felt, as if his own emotion had been torn from his gut and amplified back at him 47,000 times.

With five minutes to go to kick-off the teams came out on to the pitch. The explosion of noise which greeted the home side as they emerged from the tunnel never failed to move him. It spoke to something atavistic in him, to the fantasy of leading men into battle. Many men. Russian hordes. Wave after wave of them. It made him feel that with these supporters behind him he could win wars and conquer continents. He went to take his seat at the back of the directors' box with the most ridiculous lump in his throat. It was understood that he always sat there, in the back row, where it was more difficult for the TV cameras to pick him out. He was fully aware that they were trained on him, but they couldn't get an angle on him if he positioned himself in that left-hand corner. Next to him sat Sasha. Sasha was loyal. Sasha was the only one he allowed to sit beside him. Sasha was his fixer. Sasha had been there from the beginning. 'Never ask about the first million,' they used to say in Russia. Sasha was one of the very few who knew about Oleg's first million. Sasha was discreet. He knew when to keep quiet and when to put a consoling hand on Oleg's arm. Sasha was the one he embraced on the delirious occasions when the boys actually scored.

The teams lined up, the referee blew his whistle, and, to a crescendo of noise, the game was in progress. There were ninety agonising minutes ahead, in which Oleg would play every pass of each of his players, make every tackle, take every shot with them, bending his body this way and that in tortured sympathy with their efforts. Limb thudded into limb, boot into boot: it was the sheer physicality of the encounter that took your breath away. Sometimes the ball was thwacked, occasionally it was caressed, all at a ferocious speed. And Oleg lived every collision, railed at the randomness of every outcome, at the matter of centimetres which determined whether a passage of play flourished or frustrated his players, and marvelled at the rare moments when it all went right.

At half time the score was 0-0. He went back in drained. Why weren't they ahead? Alves had hit the post when it seemed easier to score. And then Igor had been put through on his own, one on one with the goalkeeper, the whole stadium had risen from its seats in anticipation of the goal, and the shot had bounced off the advancing goalkeeper's knee for an anticlimactic corner. Guillermo should be out there. Guillermo wouldn't have missed that chance. The opposition wasn't very good. They were in the bottom half of the table, and Oleg's team were second, one point behind the leaders. The season was almost over: there were only two games still left to play. That was why they had to win today, to stand any chance of ending up champions. A draw would be no good. No good at all. He helped himself to another shot of vodka to dull the pain.

As the second half kicked off, he felt his hand close round the metal object in his pocket. It was the miniature icon of Christ Pantocrator that his grandmother had given him all those years ago. Its edges had become worn with anxious, imprecatory handling. If he squeezed it three times, everything would be all right. The thing about football was that its uncertainty brought out the primitive, superstitious Russian in him. Score, score, score. In the second minute, Igor very nearly did, he beat the goalkeeper with a header but a defender hacked it off the line. And then, ten minutes into the half, the opposition team were awarded a free kick thirty yards out. The defensive wall formed up, a line of highly-paid athletes intent for the moment on two things: protecting their goal, and protecting their private parts from the impact of a football flying at them at sixty miles an hour. The opposition free kick taker struck the ball with fearsome power, it hit the side of the head of one of the wall of home defenders and ricocheted ineluctably into the opposite corner of the goal from the one the goalkeeper was covering. It was a total fluke, a chance in a hundred. The small band of away supporters in the corner of the stadium went wild with delight, a mini earthquake of blue. All the rest of the stadium was quiet, stunned into disbelieving silence. Every so often, shit like this happened. An opposing team, with manifestly less money and weaker players than his team, would fluke a result against his men. It was intolerable. It had to be stopped.

In the early days of his career if something had gone against him, he had people to see to the problem, to take steps to make sure it didn't go wrong again. Rivals who stood in his way were discouraged from impeding him. If they were obstinate they were removed. Occasionally someone got hurt, as a lesson to the others. But you couldn't do that with football, not now it was all so high-profile. You couldn't arrange for opposition players to meet with car accidents on dark nights. Shooting a member of the UEFA Disciplinary Committee if a judgement went against one of your own players wasn't an option either. But there were moments when he was tempted. Sorely tempted.

And now his boys were losing 1-0. At home. A sick emptiness afflicted him. If they didn't win this, his whole week would be blighted. He wouldn't be able to sleep for thinking about it. That steel deal, which was going to make him 500 million dollars this week, would taste very bitter without the victory today. Would he not trade the whole steel deal for two goals now? He clutched the icon in his pocket again, turned it over in his palm. There are moments of self-recognition in every human being's life. This was one of them. The truth was he'd let the steel deal go. He really would. When you were as rich as Oleg, the actual financial power of money lost its significance. Whether something cost 50 thousand dollars or 50 million dollars was irrelevant. All he measured anything by was how much pleasure it brought him. Right now the steel deal would bring him less pleasure than two goals going into the opposition net in the next twenty minutes. There was the answer.

When Guillermo came on as a substitute and scored in the 76th minute, part of Oleg thought he was going to weep with gratitude and the other part thought, why? Why do I have to be put through this suffering? I am one of the twenty richest men in the western hemisphere, and yet I must be subjected to this torture. No matter how much money I spend, I cannot be protected from it. When Guillermo was tripped in the penalty area in the 89th minute and Marco scored the resultant penalty, Oleg danced in Sasha's arms. The relief. The intense, all-pervasive relief, as the final whistle blew. It got to him, this kind of thing. Ridiculous, but it really got to him.

He decided to go down to the dressing room. He didn't go down after every match, but he felt the need to go today. To express his gratitude and his appreciation to the boys. To his boys. For enabling him to sleep tonight. 'Guillermo!' he greeted the goalscorer, who was sitting on the treatment table in his shorts, having a calf massaged. '*Va bene?*' '*Va bene,*' confirmed Guillermo with a slow smile. He was a dream of a striker, but he wasn't that bright. The next player he encountered was the only Englishman in the team. Barry. He was standing there thoughtfully, swathed in a towel, his hand clutching a can of expensive deodorant. 'Congratulations, Barry,' he said. 'But the victory – this we left till late.'

Barry nodded. 'The lads are over the moon. Fair play to our opponents, though, they kept battling.'

Oleg could never quite banish the suspicion that his players minded less about winning than he did. After all, they still got paid large amounts of money regardless of the result. But tonight he liked the camaraderie down here. He liked the steam and the banter and the bodies and the comforting, clichéd phrases that players like Barry spouted to him. They were just formulaic, verbal patterns that footballers learned by reading the quotations of other footballers as reproduced in tabloid newspapers and repeating them, infinitely extending their sterility. But there was a charm to them. They were like remembered lines of the most beautiful poetry when you had just won a game with a goal in the eighty-ninth minute.

'When they scored, I was beginning to be worried,' confessed Oleg.

Barry averred that the lads had themselves been gutted. But, he added, to be fair they hadn't let their heads drop. He offered the insight that the lads had run their socks off to get back into the game.

Oleg put a friendly hand on his shoulder and moved on. The whole thing moved him close to tears.

As Oleg was being driven home after the game his number one personal mobile rang. He always answered this mobile, because only the people he wanted to hear from had its number. It was Grun, his number one money man. He made it a rule to take Grun's calls.

'Oleg, it's the Jeff Koons opportunity. You asked me to remind you. Do you want to bid?'

Koons. For a moment his mind went blank. Was Koons the striker or the midfield player? 'What's the price?'

'In the region of 50 million.'

50 million. 50 million was serious. What he didn't like was being offered players for 15 million. It was an in-between kind of price. Too little for a player who would really make a difference, but too much for a young one who was still only promising. But 50 million was *galacticos* territory. 'Remind me: what's his position?'

'It says here he's an appropriationist.'

'What, some kind of box-to-box midfielder?'

'Box-to-box? I'm not good on these technical terms, Oleg.'

'A ball-winner. Maybe that's what we need. Where's he from? Bayern Munich?'

'I don't have that information.'

'Koons, Koons. Could be from the east. I like Eastern Europeans. They have good work ethic.'

'So you want to go with it?'

'Does Franz like him?' The coach's opinion must be taken into account of course. Franz had just presided over three victories in a row. Even if Franz hadn't started with Guillermo today.

'Franz?'

'Yes, Franz.'

'Oleg, I'm not sure. Why would Franz have a view on a sculpture by Jeff Koons?'

When he had to, Oleg could think quickly. It was what made him formidable. 'Just kidding you. When's the sale?'

'Monday evening. New York.'

'I'll have another look at the catalogue and get back to you.'

Oleg had turned to art partly in order to distract himself from football. Actually, there was a certain symmetry between the two, in financial terms at least. For the price of a promising, but not yet fully-established central defender – say 10 million - he could buy a reasonably good but not totally exceptional work by Gerhardt Richter. And the price structure continued to run in parallel even at the topmost echelons. If you wanted to announce yourself in the football world, if you wanted to be taken seriously, if you wanted your team to be mentioned in the same breath as Barcelona or Bayern Munich or Real Madrid, you had to be prepared to compete for the signatures of marquee players, the *galacticos*, the world stars. This meant not being afraid to spend 50 million or more on a single footballer. Once you had done that, you had definitely arrived.

Now he was being asked to spend 50 million on a sculpture in order to achieve a similar level of eminence in art. Oleg flipped open his laptop and summoned details of the Jeff Koons coming up for sale on Monday. It was entitled 'Balloon Dog'. Apparently this sculpture was 'nothing short of the Holy Grail for collectors and art foundations', or so the auction house catalogue assured him. It went on. 'In private hands the work has always communicated the prominence and stature of its owner. To own this work immediately positions the buyer alongside the very top collectors in the world and transforms a collection to an unparalleled level of greatness.' Oleg was intrigued. It was exactly what he felt he had achieved for his football team by buying Guillermo.

Yes, he liked the idea of his art collection being transformed to an unparalleled level of greatness by the simple expedient of paying 50 million for a Koons. Also, he reminded himself that you could always re-sell a work of art, generally at a profit after five or ten years, which was rarely the case with a footballer after the same period. He looked again at the image of the balloon dog. It was just a shiny dog. A shiny dog in a funny colour. It left him totally cold. On the other hand Ivana would probably like it, so he fired off an email instructing Grun to go up to 60 million. All things considered, it was stupid not to.

But dear God, that goal. And in the 89th minute. He sighed gratefully and squeezed the little silver icon in his pocket three more times.

# An Honourable
# Deception
## Paris, 1819

## Monday 1 October

The first thing I notice about the man is his nonchalance. He stands waiting in the hallway with his hands in his pockets, whistling to himself. I watch him silently from the landing above, wondering what he's up to. He shouldn't be here, of course, not in this part of the house; but what I'm more worried by is his deliberately carefree air. It's an act, a cover for something. People aren't carefree in this house. No-one carefree has any business here.

'Monsieur Moreau?' I call out gently. How I move and speak in this situation is important. I descend the stairs in unhurried but purposeful steps. 'Can I help you?' I add halfway down, trying to keep my voice calm but authoritative. To my own ear I sound for a moment comically like a hotelkeeper. But that's what I am in a way. Moreau is a guest in my house, a paying guest. And I am his keeper.

He looks up and smiles at me. I smile back, relieved that he's responding to my calmness. Moreau is in his early sixties, running distinctly to fat. There is no polite way to describe his face. It's bulbous. There are bags under his eyes, his jowl sags, and his nose has the surface consistency of a strawberry. But still an air of prosperity clings to him, something to do with the cut of his coat, the quality of his shoes, the ring he wears on his little finger. In the world outside this house he is a man of standing and means, a merchant of jewellery with three successful shops in Paris. On top of that, he's taken trouble with his toilet today: he's brushed his hair and he's freshly shaved. The barber must have been in already this morning. That's one way this household is different from a real hotel: you can't let the guests loose with their own razors.

'Thought I'd wander downstairs,' says Moreau in explanation. His manner is unusually bluff, even hearty. 'I fancy I might take a walk today.'

'Good, excellent,' I say. This is certainly progress. It's the first time the man's been at all forthcoming about anything. Since his arrival ten days ago all he's done is sit in his bedroom, immobile, pensive, closed in on himself. He's been perfectly polite when spoken to, but totally uncommunicative about the events that have brought him here. 'Perhaps you might like a turn in the garden?' I suggest. 'It's stopped raining now, and there are still some very beautiful roses out.'

44

'Roses?' The idea seems to throw him for a moment. Then he makes a determined effort to regain his composure. 'Roses,' he repeats gruffly. 'Yes, perhaps a little later.'

'As you wish.'

He walks over to the table and drums his fingers on the polished top. There's clearly still something on his mind, though he's trying to hide it, to recapture the cover of his initial nonchalance. When he looks up, he seems to have succeeded, because he's smiling again. He says, 'It's about that time in the morning, isn't it?'

I don't know what he's talking about, so I smile back at him.

'As I was passing, I thought I might as well have a look for myself,' he continues.

'Of course.'

He goes on standing there. He's stopped drumming his fingers on the table and started rubbing his hands together, rubbing them together slightly too fast. Finally he says in a voice that can no longer disguise its concern, 'They'd come through this door, wouldn't they?'

'Are you expecting visitors?'

'No, no, no.' A cloud of irritation crosses the sun of his affability. 'I mean, they'd be delivered here, wouldn't they?'

'Forgive me: what would?'

'My letters, my dear fellow, my letters.'

'Ah, your letters.' I hesitate, then decide to be honest: 'I'm very sorry, I don't believe that anything has actually been received for you today.'

'There's nothing for me?' Moreau's features register total mystification. His eyebrows go to meet each other, and his mouth opens in a lopsided caricature of incredulity. I am constantly struck by the mobility of people's faces here, the way emotions in their nudity achieve an extra power of expressiveness.

'Not this morning, no.'

'That's *very* strange.' The emphasis on the second word signals his awareness of the machinations of shadowy but cunning opponents, and his vigilance against them.

'Were you expecting a particular letter?'

'Well of course I was.'

'Could I ask who it was from?'

An unexpected look of sly self-satisfaction crosses Moreau's face. 'From a lady, as a matter of fact.'

'Ah. From a lady.'

Not from Madame Moreau, it seems. How strange. I nod sympathetically. At least Moreau's talking to me, telling me things, things he's chosen up till now to keep hidden. This is what I need to work with, raw material that I can begin to interpret in order to help him. Medicine of the mind is no different from medicine of the body, it's a question of diagnosing inner states from outer signs. And once you've got a plausible diagnosis, you can begin a more effective treatment.

'Who exactly is the lady?' I ask.

Moreau frowns. 'I'm surprised to hear you ask that question, Dr Esquirol.'

'I'm sorry. I didn't intend to intrude in any way.'

'I couldn't possibly tell you her name. There's her honour to be considered.'

'No, of course.'

He sighs again and gestures to the front door. 'Are you sure nothing came this morning?'

'Absolutely sure, I'm afraid.'

'Could someone have tampered with the post? Removed my letter while it was waiting on the hall table?'

'No. I keep a strict surveillance on what arrives in this house and what happens to it afterwards.'

Moreau closes his eyes and shrugs his shoulders, more in sadness than in anger. 'It's fairly clear what's going on here, you know,' he says.

'What's going on?'

'It stands to reason. They must be preventing her from writing to me.'

Who are 'they'? But I don't ask. 'These things aren't easy for anyone,' I say.

'Under the circumstances, I feel I should go to her?' The sentence starts as a statement and ends as a question.

I take his arm gently but firmly. 'Not now, I think. Perhaps better later. See how you feel in a day or two.'

'A day or two.' Moreau nods, and allows himself to be guided back upstairs. All at once he seems almost relieved. His eyes, which were fiery with passion a few moments ago, have dulled. 'Now you mention it,' he says, 'I must confess I'm feeling a little tired.'

'It's understandable. You have not been well. You must rest as much as possible.'

He pauses on the landing, then raises a finger of resolution. 'I know what I'll do. I'll write her another letter. This afternoon. At least I can keep her spirits up, even if her letters aren't getting through to me.'

'Good idea.'

I open the bedroom door and help him to lie down on his bed, removing his shoes, arranging his pillows and settling him as comfortably as I can. Then I draw up a chair and sit in silence for a moment, watching him, and thinking about his case.

It is fourteen days since Moreau was found by the police in the small hours of the morning, wandering the embankment of the Seine. It was a cold night, but he was totally naked. No, he wasn't drunk. He was surprisingly lucid, even matter of fact, when apprehended, entirely understanding that the officers were only doing their duty in taking him into temporary custody. He was sorry, but he didn't know where his clothes had gone or how he'd lost them. So his worried family committed him here, to my house in the rue de Buffon, where I run my private sanatorium. And since that time, even in those rational moments between passages of incoherence, he's steadfastly refused to explain himself. Whenever I ask him anything about that evening by the Seine, he replies - a trifle huffily - that it's a private matter, and he can't discuss it further. I've been content to leave it, because at first new patients need calm, to allow them peace and space, to isolate them from their familiar domestic surroundings. That way I can gradually build a new perspective for them on their problems. That's the next step in the healing of their minds.

And now there's progress. Today he's begun to confide in me. He's told me about this lady he writes letters to, who may or may not be his mistress, who may or may not be the root of his mental distress. I shift softly in my chair and sit on in silence for a while, because I don't want to rush things, but equally I don't want to miss the opportunity that seems to be opening up.

'And can you remember anything about what happened that night?' I ask in a gentle voice.

'What night was that?'

'That night when they found you down by the river. When you were taken into custody by the police.'

His eyes have misted over again. 'I really don't know what you're talking about. I'm sorry, my dear fellow, I'm afraid I can't help you there at all.'

I leave him to rest and go down to my study. I need to record developments, to write up my notes on Moreau while what he's just said and done are fresh in my memory.

Of course I don't yet know enough about the details of Moreau's case to be sure what exactly drove him to remove his clothes and wander the late-night streets of Paris naked. But my hypothesis is that some disturbance of the emotions, very possibly to do with this mysterious lady correspondent, has led to a false association of ideas, to a localised malfunctioning of the man's reason. That makes it another case of monomania. Monomania. I have invented the term because it explains the symptoms of many patients I have seen over the years. It explains them, at least, even if it doesn't always lead to a cure. But it's only by reading the outward symptoms that you can decode the inner cause. It's the first stage in a process.

Moreau's case is a monomania because it's a partial madness. The mental disturbance seems to relate to a single subject only. In most other ways Moreau's reason functions normally. That's typical. Much of the time you can hold deceptively intelligent conversations with the man, like just now. You don't know he's disturbed unless you engage with him in the one distinct area of his madness. I've seen it with many other patients, like the kleptomaniac schoolmaster who was in all other ways an excellent teacher but kept stealing his pupils' possessions from them, or the mild-mannered tailor who made excellent jackets but was convinced that he commanded Napoleon's Imperial Bodyguard, or the exemplary mother of four children who couldn't leave her house because she believed that flocks of birds were gathering in the trees to attack her.

'I know you're God's gift to the medical profession, my dear Dr Esquirol,' my wife said to me yesterday, 'but is it necessary for you to work quite as hard as you do?' She treats me with a mixture of cynicism, fondness, and mild amusement that has evolved over twenty years of marriage. It's good for me not to be taken too seriously by my wife, or so she tells me. 'I sometimes wonder if you don't love your cases more than you love me,' she went on. 'But you're lucky: I'm not a jealous woman. And I suppose that things could be worse if my only rival is your work.'

Anne's right. Not that I love my work more than I love her, but that it does absorb me. All my professional life I've studied the medicine of the mind. I've got my own pupils now, at the Salpêtrière hospital where I direct the care of the insane. And some years ago Anne and I took the lease on this large mansion in the Rue de Buffon, appropriately positioned next door on the one side to the Salpêtrière itself and on the other to the Jardin des Plantes, near where they've opened a zoo of exotic animals. She and I run a private home here, where more privileged members of society can move in to receive the sort of discreet treatment for their mental ailments that's impossible in the public wards of the Salpêtrière or the Bicêtre. I couldn't do it without her. She seems to thrive on running this hotel for the disturbed, dining with them, caring for them, living out with them their advances and their setbacks. The point is we've never had children, so our marriage is founded on my work. If she didn't share in my absorption, we would not be as happy as we are.

I'm a lucky man, of course I am. I am an explorer, a pioneer cutting a way through an unknown jungle, a mapmaker of the human mind. That means I have to draw new boundaries, to identify hitherto undiscovered landmarks, to invent names for them. It's a dark continent that I find myself charting, but it's a varied and fascinating one. Anne tells me I sound pompous, and I probably do, but now and then I like to remind my pupils that what we're studying rises higher than the mere mechanics of the body. Although it's rooted in physiology, insanity affects the very principle and source of intelligent life. These are momentous landscapes that I have the privilege to survey.

## Wednesday 3 October

On the slightly elevated dais at one end of the large salon, a trio of musicians are making final preparations for their recital. I watch them with a faint impatience. The violinist is tuning up, his long prehensile fingers moving up and down the strings with a febrile elegance, while the flautist and the harpsichordist adjust stands and set up sheet music with studied expressions of professional concentration.

'Are you ready, gentlemen?' I call across to them. The violinist nods with apparent composure. But as he does so, he casts a cautious eye in the direction of the main doors leading to the dining room. I walk across and pull them open to admit the audience.

The cluster of convalescent patients, helped by their servants and attendants, begin to shuffle in and take their seats on the chairs that have been arranged to face the performers. There is a perceptible anticipation, an undercurrent of nervous tension and heightened emotion. Someone drops his walking stick and the woman next to him gives a little shriek of excited laughter. I move quickly across to pick up the stick and calm things down. These musical evenings are my own innovation. I am convinced of the therapeutic value of music to troubled minds, and these weekly events have become eagerly awaited by our little community. But they have to be carefully planned and supervised. It's important not to let things get out of hand. So not everyone attends: some are either too ill or too sunk in gloom to leave their rooms. Others are too unstable to be risked. The musicians are steeled against the occasional eruption of emotion from the audience, but if too many people have to be carried out weeping, screaming, or laughing it spoils the pleasure for the rest.

Finally everyone is in place. The violinist steps forward and announces the first piece: Cimarosa, which is always a popular choice. A polite ripple of applause, and the music begins: charming, light-hearted, serene. Surreptitiously I allow my gaze to wander the audience. At first sight you could almost imagine this is a normal musical soirée in someone's private house. Until you look closer at the faces. Some are enrapt, moving gently in time with the melody. Others are lost in their own thoughts: distracted, anxious, transfixed. There is Moreau, one plump leg crossed over the other, leaning back frowning; or his neighbour, a thin young man with a prominent Adam's apple, who is concentrating very hard on observing his own nose from different angles, shutting first one eye then the other; or his neighbour in turn, an elderly white-haired lady down whose cheeks course tears of unfeigned pleasure.

It's a good concert. After the prettiness of Cimarosa we have some Mozart, and then finish with Haydn. It is music chosen to calm the passions rather than to inflame them. I try to ease my own anxieties by concentrating on it. Gradually I relax. I imagine the human body as essentially an assemblage of more or less taut fibres, upon which the music produced by the vibration of the strings of the keyboard resonates with the same mellifluous effect.

Just after nine o'clock the last piece draws to a close and the performers come forward to the edge of the dais to bow to enthusiastic applause. Then they withdraw and the audience shuffles out towards the stairs and their bedrooms. Heads nod in approval. Others dab moist eyes with handkerchiefs and blow their noses. As the last stragglers disappear, I am aware of one man lingering.

It is Moreau. He is staring at the engraving above the fireplace in the flickering candlelight, apparently absorbed in it.

'Did you enjoy the concert?' I ask him.

He waves a dismissive hand. 'Excellent, excellent.'

'What are you looking at?'

'My eye was caught by the print up here. I can't quite make out its subject in this light.'

'It's a scene from classical history. Antiochus and Stratonice.'

'Lovers, were they?'

'Yes. Antiochus was the son of Seleucus, King of Thrace, and Stratonice was the wife of...'

I stop because Moreau is no longer listening to me. He is reaching into his breast pocket and pulling out a newly-sealed envelope. He is suddenly animated, almost feverish. 'I'd be grateful if you could have this delivered for me,' he says in a low, urgent voice. 'It needs to be handled with absolute discretion.' He touches his nose with a significant gesture whose exaggeration makes it unintentionally comic.

I sense that I am on trial, that my good faith is being put to the test. I take it without allowing my gaze to fall upon the name on the envelope. But the expression on Moreau's face, which combines anxiety with a certain sly self-congratulation, is not difficult to read. 'Of course,' I say, putting the letter away carefully in my own pocket.

We turn away from the fireplace. The print is forgotten. Moreau gives a little cough, flicks a small piece of dust off the lapel of his jacket, and adds with an affectation of casualness: 'Should get there tomorrow, I suppose?'

'Is it for delivery within Paris?'

'Of course it is.' The impatience bubbles to the surface.

'In that case you could certainly rely on it arriving tomorrow, yes.'

'That's good.' Moreau is brisker. 'I have no doubt that my correspondent's spirit will be considerably lightened by its receipt.' He pauses, and appears to be making further calculations. 'So I can expect a reply by the end of the week?'

'Very possibly.'

'Excellent.' Moreau nods. 'I'll bid you goodnight then, doctor.'

I usher him towards the stairs. 'Goodnight, Monsieur Moreau.'

Back in the privacy of my study I stand for a moment, thinking. My hand grasps the letter in my pocket, I feel the thick texture of the paper between my fingers. I wonder about it, weighing up what to do next. A moment later my wife comes in.

'My dearest,' I say, taking the envelope out and laying it face-down on the desk, 'I need your advice. What would you do with this if you were me?'

'What is it?' Anne asks, moving across the room to pull the curtains over the window. The candles on the fireplace flicker.

'It's a letter written by Monsieur Moreau. He has given it to me for delivery. I have reason to believe it's to his mistress.'

'What are you unsure about?'

I find myself ticking off the facts of the case on my fingers. 'My instinct is that this illicit love affair may lie at the root of Monsieur Moreau's mental distress. In order to help him I need to know more about his circumstances. At the moment he refuses to speak candidly to me. I suspect that if I read the contents of this envelope I would be in a better position to help him. Do I open it, get what I need from it, then reseal it and send it on its way? Or would that be a breach of trust?'

'You shouldn't read his letter.' She is firm on the point. 'That would be wrong. But I think you could make a note of the name of the lady concerned, and her address. Then if the need arises later you could call on her and talk with her in confidence.'

It seems a reasonable idea. I love my wife for her good sense and decisiveness. I turn the letter over and we both read the words that Moreau has written in his surprisingly firm and upright hand. '*To Mademoiselle Mars,*' it says, '*Théâtre Royal, Paris.*'

'Is this a joke?' I hear Anne exclaim. 'This is Monsieur Moreau's mistress?'

Mademoiselle Mars. The name is faintly familiar, but I can't recollect from where. 'Do you know the lady?' I ask.

'I know of her, certainly. And if you don't, my dear husband, you must be one of the very few men in Paris who are unaware of her existence. She is an extraordinarily highly-regarded actress.'

'So Mademoiselle Mars is very famous?'

'Very famous indeed. She's one of the adornments of the Paris Stage.'

'Of great beauty?'

'Exceptionally so.'

'How old is she?'

'In her late twenties, I suppose.'

'How extraordinary.' I can't help thinking of the flabby, bulbous appearance of the ageing Henri Moreau. He's not prepossessing to look at.

Anne is more matter of fact. 'Not so extraordinary. It wouldn't be the first such bargain struck between youth and old age, where one side provides the beauty and the other the wealth.'

I suppose she's right. I try to imagine myself calling on the actress to question her about her illicit relationship with Henri Moreau. It wouldn't be an easy interview. I ring the bell for my servant Joseph. When he comes I give the letter to him immediately, as if to remove all temptation from my hands as quickly as possible.

'Please make sure this letter is delivered by the earliest possible post in the morning,' I tell him.

## Friday 5 October

I hear footsteps approaching my study door, and a low but urgent knocking. 'Come in,' I call.

A forlorn figure is standing there, a forlorn figure with a deliberately casual smile playing about his lips. 'Ah, good afternoon, doctor. I was just passing so I thought I would stop to inquire if there has been any post for me today?'

'I'm sorry, Monsieur Moreau, there has been nothing.'

It is painful to watch the disappointment on the man's face, a disappointment mixed with perplexity and wounded pride. 'And the afternoon post has been delivered?'

'I am afraid so.'

Moreau shakes his head, as if to clear it of a lingering fog. He says in a thick voice, threatening tears, 'I don't understand it.'

'Monsieur Moreau,' I say gently, standing up from my chair, 'the weather is mild today. Will you take a turn in the garden with me before the light fades?'

'If... if you wish.'

At first we walk in silence. There is a mist shrouding the trees, softening their outlines. Finally I say, 'I hope you will not take it amiss, Monsieur Moreau, if I suggest something to you.'

'Please do.'

'I think it may ease your spirit to tell me a little about the lady whose letter you are awaiting.'

'The lady?' Moreau looks up sharply; for a moment it seems his anger will flare again. But he crumples suddenly, making a little movement of acquiescence with his head. 'If you wish, if you wish.'

'Am I not right in saying that your mind's been much occupied with her?'

'I can't deny it.'

'I'm not going to compromise the lady's reputation by naming her, but would I be right in assuming that she is a person of considerable fame, someone highly regarded in her own walk of life?'

'I don't know who told you this, Dr Esquirol; but yes, you're quite right.' He shrugs, not entirely displeased by the admission.

'You have my word that everything which passes between us is in confidence. I am your doctor and you are my patient.'

'I appreciate that.' A colder tone now. I sense a pause in the melting of Moreau's hostility, as if this reminder of our relationship is not to his taste.

Push on. Flatter him further. 'It can't have been easy for you to conduct relations in view of the lady's fame as a beauty, her familiarity to the public?'

Moreau kicks aside a fir cone with his buckled shoe. 'No. It hasn't been easy at all.'

'How did you first contrive to speak to her?'

There is a silence. Then Moreau murmurs in a voice suddenly vibrant with regret: 'Oh, my dear sir: would that I had!'

'You haven't spoken to her?'

'No, the opportunity hasn't yet presented itself.'

'Then how did you first meet?'

'We haven't precisely met, that's to say not in the conventional sense.'

'Forgive me: how did you become aware of your mutual... your mutual attachment if you haven't met?'

His whole face lights up. 'That's the miracle of it. From the first, her eyes sought mine. Mine, out of all those in the theatre.'

'Ah. As she acted on the stage, you mean?'

'Of course. At every performance she seeks my gaze. She searches me out from beyond the footlights. At first I watched her eyes scanning the footlights till she found me. Then, to guide her, I began always sitting in the same box. We communicate the passion we share for each other, it is understood between us. Those looks cannot lie. So I've written to her to express my feelings. I know she'll have tried to write to me in return, but her letters don't reach me. I can only assume that her enemies are intercepting them. Nonetheless she knows from my letters that my devotion to her will be undying, that she can rely on me. You see, I attended every performance she gave last month at the Théâtre Royal.'

'What play was being performed?'

'A most moving production. *Hero and Leander.*'

'And Mademoiselle Mars was playing...'

Moreau replies, in a voice once more thickening with emotion, 'Hero, of course.'

'Of course.'

I am touched by the mixture of pride, perplexity and despair with which the man lifts his hands in a wordless gesture. And all at once I understand: Hero and Leander, of course. Leander swims across the Hellespont to prove his love for Hero, who waits for him on the further shore. Where was Moreau apprehended? On the embankment of the Seine, having taken off all his clothes. He must have been about to dive into the water in emulation of Hero's lover. What power to delude is vested in the human imagination. It's fortunate that Moreau didn't actually attempt to swim: he would probably have drowned in the chill, grey waters of the river at night. Just as Leander did in the end in the Hellespont.

'But my dear sir,' I exclaim involuntarily. 'At your age! You must be careful...'

There is sweat on Moreau's upper lip. He looks grey and unwell. 'It's extraordinary, isn't it? That this beautiful woman should be so moved by me, when I'm not in the first flush of my powers, not by any means. But then I see again her look of yearning, cast at me across the footlights. Love is blind, doctor. And I know where my heart's duty lies. I must persist, for her sake. For both our sakes.'

'My poor fellow,' I say, putting a hand upon his arm. A chill wind blows through the trees in the garden. 'Come inside. It's getting cold.'

I report on my conversation with Moreau to Anne that evening. 'You see,' I explain, 'he's convinced himself that this actress loves him. But she's probably no more aware of his existence than she is of the street sweeper outside the theatre foyer.'

Anne nods thoughtfully. 'What would make Monsieur Moreau happiest, do you think, at this moment?'

'Well, I suppose it would be to receive a reply from Madame Mars. For a letter actually to arrive here from her acknowledging their love.'

'But he's not going to get one, is he?'

'Unless we produce one for him,' I suggest.

'What do you mean? Write one yourself?'

'Well, the fact is he's never actually received a letter from her so he has no idea of her handwriting. In that respect it shouldn't be difficult to make a reply from her look convincing.'

'Are you happy to do such a thing? To defraud your patient?'

'If it makes him better... it would be an honourable fraud.'

'How would it make him better to receive such a letter?'

'If it gave him certain reassurances. And led him to certain conclusions.'

'What reassurances? What conclusions?'

I explain to her what I have in mind. She looks dubious. 'It might be worth trying,' she concedes. 'If it were carried off convincingly.'

'Yes,' I agree, 'it must be convincing. That's why...'

'What?'

'That's why I thought I might ask you to write it.'

'You want *me* to write the letter?'

'In these circumstances what I fancy is called for is a woman's touch.'

'Really, my dear husband, what an extraordinary idea.'

'Will you do it, my dear?'

She doesn't reply. But she shakes her head and smiles to herself. I can see she is intrigued by my request.

The next morning she hands me a piece of paper which contains several paragraphs of her handwriting.

'What's this?'

'It's the letter that Monsieur Moreau might shortly receive, if you think it's suitable.'

*My dearest,*

*Your letters have come as sweetest balm to my troubled breast. I can no longer leave them unacknowledged, although for reasons that I will explain I have been tempted, for my heart's safety, to take that course.*

*I cannot describe what happiness it gives me to know that you have caught the looks of love which I cast to you across the footlights of the stage, to know that your gaze has indeed responded tenderly to mine. Had circumstances been different, what might we not have done together, what heights might we not have attained? But, my brave Leander, it cannot be.*

*I have been weak to allow myself, through our clandestine meetings of the eye, to reveal the nature of my feelings for you. For I have a terrible secret that prevents me ever claiming your love. The truth, my dearest, is that I suffer from a grave affliction of the heart; not the imaginary lesion so dear to the poets, but a physical weakness that is the despair of the greatest doctors in Paris. The medical experts are of one voice: if I allow myself intimacy with a man I truly love, the intensity of the feeling will be fatal to the functioning of that organ which is essential to life, and I must inevitably die.*

*Thus far, no man has touched me in such a way. But you, I sense, are different from the rest. So you and I must never meet. And you must take this terrible secret of mine with you to the grave. Share it with no-one else. I only reveal it to you because I love you.*

*I know you have a loving wife who rightly claims your loyalty. For my sake, turn to her now and do not look back to me. Be steadfast in your devotion to her. This is the noble way. And we can forever console ourselves, you and I, with the perfection of the glances that we have exchanged, the looks that have told everything, the understanding between us that needs no further elaboration. Although our lips will never have met, our souls for a few brief moments will have been perfectly entwined. Our love is offered up as a tribute to Venus, with its purity unsullied.*

*No more letters from you now. Let it be. If you love me, come to me no more. At best it will make me sadder than I can bear. At worst it will kill me. Show no-one this letter. Know only that you have won my poor, frail heart and be content.*

*Yours,* in silentio aeternitatis,

*M. Mars*

'It's brilliant,' I tell her.

She shrugs. 'It had to be done properly.'

'That last touch, *in the silence of eternity*. It's inspired.'

'You think that Monsieur Moreau will accept this letter as genuine?'

'I don't know. But I do know that there are times when the human mind will believe something to be true against all likelihood, simply because it wants it to be true.'

'And derive comfort from it?'

'I hope so, in this case.'

'So in this case the deception is what you call an honourable one.'

'I believe so.' I fold the letter into the envelope. 'There now, to complete the effect please address it.'

She writes, 'To Monsieur Henri Moreau, Rue de Buffon'.

'Thank you, I shall give it to him in the morning.'

## Thursday 11 October

This morning Moreau leaves our sanatorium. There is no denying that his recovery has been remarkable. I go to bid him farewell and find him standing in the hall again, near the table where he once waited forlornly for his letters. This time, however, he looks a different man: sleek and confident as he directs the servants who are carrying his trunk out of the front door to the waiting carriage. 'Careful of that. I said don't bang the corners! That's right, easy does it.'

'It's good to see you so much better,' I say to him.

'Feel in good fettle. Finally thrown off that fever. And the headaches have gone.'

'That's excellent.' I have noticed before that my patients are much happier to ascribe their suffering to physical causes, to see themselves as victims of an illness of the body rather than of the mind. It is what they understand, what makes sense to them.

'Very grateful to you for your care and all that,' goes on Moreau. 'But frankly I shan't be sorry to be home. Can't leave the women in charge of the household for too long, eh? Who knows what mischief they'll get up to?'

I shake him by the hand and wish him well. I am tempted innocently to inquire if he ever got the letter he was hoping for; to probe whether its contents were satisfactory. But the patient's present high spirits are presumably testament to that. Anne stands next to me as we wave him off and watch his carriage disappearing down the Rue de Buffon.

'You are truly a remarkable woman,' I tell her. 'Your gift with words is yet one more of your many talents. I'm sure if you wanted you could be a poet, or at least a writer of novels.'

'I thought you didn't approve of novels?'

I am on the point of reiterating my belief that imaginative invention can sometimes be abused, that those who write novels are often insufficiently aware of the dangerous power they wield, a power to pervert sensibility, to excite unreal and violent sentiments, leading to a host of nervous complaints, in women particularly. But then I realise that she's teasing me so I kiss her on the forehead and say with a little humorous sniff, 'I'm sure that if you wrote one, my dearest, its effect upon the reader would be nothing but beneficial.'

## Friday 19 October

Today, eight days on from Moreau's departure, I receive a letter from Madame Moreau. It thanks me again for what I did for her husband while he was under my care. It remarks upon the unusually good spirits that Monsieur Moreau has been in since he returned home. Which makes what has just happened all the more inexplicable, all the harder to accept. Because yesterday morning, the letter informs me, Monsieur Moreau went out for a short walk. And early in the evening, after he hadn't returned and a search had been made, Monsieur Moreau's body was found floating in the cold and swollen waters of the Seine.

What is this news but one more medical phenomenon, one more scientific fact, one more symptom to be classified and recorded? I put the letter down on my desk, select a new nib, and reach for my notes.

# Pretty Little Jug

Extract from the Diary of Evelyn Waugh:

*Croatia, Sunday 16 July 1944*

>*We got into aeroplane – a large Dakota transport – at nightfall [in Bari]. Randolph, Philip Jordan, I, Air Commodore Carter, some Jugoslav partisans (one girl), two or three Russians added at the last moment... we flew in darkness, noisy, uncomfortable, dozing sometimes. After some hours I was conscious by my ears that we were descending and circling the airfield, then we suddenly shot upwards and the next thing I knew was that I was walking in a cornfield by the light of the burning aeroplane talking to a strange British officer about the progress of the war in a detached fashion and that he was saying 'You'd better sit down for a bit skipper.'*

Funny, that. To come across yourself in the context of someone else's diary, so many years later. Mine is hardly a conspicuous role in Waugh's account of the events of that day and night: 'some

Jugoslav partisans (one girl)'. I am dismissed in parentheses as just a lone, anonymous female. And he couldn't even get that right. The bit about being female, I mean. Not at that stage, anyway. Ah well. So is history written.

I was recruited to British Intelligence in early 1944 by a man called Major Makins whom I met in a bar in Brindisi. He was a clever, well-meaning fellow but a catastrophic communicator, being congenitally incapable of completing his sentences. The only way to make progress in our conversation was for me to finish them for him.

'How long have you been… um…. knocking around in this… um…. neck of … um… neck of…'

'The woods?'

'The woods, precisely.'

I told him I'd come out to Greece in 1932 and had been drifting around the Balkans ever since. Three months ago I'd got across to liberated Italy on a fishing boat.

'So you know the natives pretty well over there? The… um… the…'

'The Jugoslavs?'

'That's it. The Jugs.'

I'd forgotten the deep-seated British need to reduce all foreigners to buffoonery by means of comic nicknames. 'Yes, I think you could say I know the 'Jugs' pretty well,' I told him.

'And do you have a British…. A British um…. um….'

'Umbrella?'

'Um… no, er… Passport?'

I said I did. He told me I might be just the sort of chap he was looking for. Was I prepared to do something to help the allied war effort? Why not, I thought? Most of the big decisions of my life have been made on impulse. So Makins arranged some training for me, and I learned how to operate a wireless. I found that a career which had so far included being an artist, an acrobat, a monk and a goatherd equipped me surprisingly well for war service. In addition to that, a facility for languages (I spoke Greek and Serbo-Croat like a native) and a predilection for dressing in women's clothing qualified me perfectly for a role in military espionage.

I was born Adrian Lush in 1909 in a south-eastern suburb of London. I was good at drawing and studied at the Slade in the later 1920s. After that I joined a travelling circus as a trainee trapeze artist. On tour to Greece and the Balkans I converted to the Greek orthodox church and spent three years as a novitiate monk in a monastery on Patmos, before realising that what I really wanted to be was a landscape painter after all. In the years before the war I supported myself by working at various resorts on the Dalmatian coast as a waiter and water-skiing instructor, and exhibiting occasionally in London. In those days I had a slim dapper figure and a remarkable physical agility. Nina Hamnett spoke of my 'elfin beauty', which was kind of the old girl.

In fact, as the years went by I lived in an increasingly uncomfortable relationship with my own body. I found I was only truly at ease when dressed as a woman. I thought more clearly, behaved more naturally. Yes, Brother Adrian the monk and

Adrian Lush the water-skier were male; but since the German occupation of Dalmatia I had been living an isolated rural life working on a farm, answering if challenged mostly to the name of Adriana, the shepherdess. I hovered between the genders, adapting to what I thought I could get away with. In Italy I had become male again. Provisionally. Until I saw the lie of the land.

Makins had a plan, which he explained to me. I was to go back to mainland Jugoslavia and infiltrate myself into a partisan unit, posing as a Croat. I said that I was willing to undertake the mission, but I wanted to do it as a woman. Makins looked troubled and asked me if I was sure. A female Jug? Absolutely, I said. They would trust me more readily than if I presented myself to them out of the blue as a man. So at the beginning of April I was landed clandestinely on the coast above Dubrovnik, and made my way to the town of Ploce where I was to encounter – as if by chance - the unit of my new comrades. Allied Intelligence gave me to believe I would find them there, a band of twenty or so partisans under the command of two men called Petr and Ilic, conducting guerrilla warfare against the occupying German forces.

For once Allied Intelligence had got it right. It worked. I arrived in Ploce and found Petr and Ilic drinking in the town square. My story was that I had come on foot from a village called Listica twenty miles away, recently laid waste by the retreating Germans. I told Petr and Ilic that all my family had been wiped out in the onslaught, and now my only ambition in life was to kill as many Germans as possible. The partisans in Ploce accepted me. They accepted me as a Croat, and they accepted me as a woman. As I say, by then I found dressing as a female came very naturally to me. I had grown my hair long, and I used deft touches of mascara round my eyes; occasionally even lipstick. Nothing fancy: most of the time I wore trousers and boots like the men. My only little female vanity was the scarf I wound round my head and tied with an unobtrusive chic. You know what undermines the authenticity of most female impersonators? The size of their hands and feet. Those are what give them away. But mine were small, delicate, graceful, though I say it myself. Thus, Petr and Ilic and the others recruited me into the unit. Not that they made many concessions to my femininity, and I worked as hard as any man. In retrospect, perhaps I got on better with Petr than with Ilic. Petr was the easy-going one, whereas Ilic was a man of few words and a brutal temper. I was known as Adriana, but more often simply as Comrade. That was how they thought of me, first as a comrade, and only secondarily as a woman.

One other thing that made me valuable to them was that I spoke English. I explained I had learned the language teaching water-skiing to British tourists during pre-war summers in resorts along the Dalmatian coast. They were impressed by this, so that when Petr and Ilic were invited to a meeting with Allied Intelligence in Bari to attempt a co-ordination of Partisan operations on the mainland, they took me with them. The three of us crossed by fishing boat to Vis, the allied-held island off the Croatian coast, and from there we were flown on to Italy.

I had a separate clandestine meeting with Makins in Bari, unknown to Petr and Ilic. What was I able to tell him?

Probably not much more than he knew already. I confirmed that the short-term war aims of the partisans were aligned with those of the allies in as much as they both wanted to defeat the Germans, to push them out of Jugoslavia as soon as possible. But the partisans were simultaneously fighting a civil war against the Ustashe, the bloodthirsty Croatian fanatics who had had German support. The first allegiance of my partisan friends was to Tito, the communist: they had no time for the monarchy. How close did I feel were the Partisans to the So…. So… Soviets, Makins asked me? I told him that on the ground so-called Russian military advisers were very much in evidence, incorporated into partisan units. If the western allies were expecting post-war Jugoslavia to settle down into a nice sensible liberal monarchy, they were going to be disappointed. But then who was I, one-time trapeze artist and Greek orthodox monastic, latterly water-skiing drag-queen and hermit shepherdess, to read the runes for Makins?

'Still working OK, is it? Your um… your um…. your um… ?'

'My disguise?'

'That's it.'

I repeated my belief that the partisans were more prepared to trust me as a woman. That it had been easier to win their confidence.

'I've always felt that on an op. like this the best judge is the… um… the…'

'The agent himself?' I hazarded.

'Precisely.' He looked at me earnestly. 'Want to go back, Lush?' he asked. 'You don't have to you know, it's not... um... you know...'

'Mandatory? No, I'd like to. One more time.'

'Good man,' said Makins. He could manage two-word sentences. But I could see the uncertainty in his eyes as I shook hands with him in farewell. Should he have said 'Good woman'?

Reading that entry in the Waugh diaries brought it all back with unexpected vividness. There was a breeze from the sea that warm July evening in Bari when we assembled at the military airfield and stood in the lee of the large Dakota awaiting embarkation for the flight back to Vis. At last, we were told to pile in. There was not much space for passengers as the plane was already packed with cargo. The Air Commodore and the two British Commando officers were grouped at the front, and inferior personnel took their places sitting on their luggage further down, in descending order of importance. Petr, Ilic and I were thus pretty near the back.

An hour or so into the flight one of the two British officers manoeuvred his way carefully down the plane distributing peaches to the disparate assembly of Russians, partisans and other ranks propped against the sides of the aircraft. There was something about him that annoyed me. It was the self-conscious largesse of his actions. Look at me, they said, at ease with the proletariat. Am I not the perfect example of *noblesse oblige*? He paused in front of me as he gave me my peach. His breath smelt heavily of brandy.

'Would you like me to skin it for you?' he said in a manner simultaneously lordly and suggestive.

'That I can do for myself,' I said. In English, but with an assumed Croatian accent.

'Ah, my dear girl, but the trick is to do it one-handed. Can you manage that?'

'I have never tried.'

'Once you master that skill you hold the key to an infinity of pleasure. Your husband will be a happy man.'

He stood there for a moment, looking at me, as if expecting congratulation on his wit, gratitude for his generosity, and acknowledgement of his own supreme wonderfulness. He was a pretty repulsive figure, overweight, florid, dissolute. Then he turned and staggered back up to the front of the plane. There is something about the British aristocracy. Even in the action of staggering they still manage to convey an arrogance and self-satisfaction. It reminded me of why I had long since chosen to live abroad.

Petr cupped his hand to his mouth and shouted into my ear over the noise of the engines: 'Know who that is?'

'No?'

'He is the son of Winston Churchill.'

'You're joking.'

'I am serious. And I think he wants to get into your pants, comrade.'

'He'd better not try.'

'Perhaps there would be political advantage to our cause if you let him.'

'No, comrade. Don't even consider it.'

'Be a little nice to him. See what you can get out of him.'

I considered the duplicities of espionage. Here was I pretending to these partisans that I was a native of the village of Listica when I had been born and brought up in Beckenham, that I was committed to the cause of Jugoslav communism when I was working for British intelligence, that I was a woman when I was a man; and here they were suggesting to me that, as a woman, I should sleep with the son of the prime minister of my own country in order to compromise him and thereby usher in a glorious new socialist state to the Balkans. Thus was I to play my part in altering the course of history.

I watched the son of the British prime minister reach his place up near the cockpit and lower himself heavily into a sitting position facing the other British officer, who was steadfastly reading a book. Churchill junior took a long swig from his flask then said something to his friend, who put down his book and peered scowling in my direction before beginning to read again. I didn't like the look of this other officer any more than Churchill. He had a very red face, with pig eyes and a small bristling moustache above a tight, discontented mouth. In retrospect, I suppose he was Evelyn Waugh.

I remember our descent towards the airfield of Vis. I stood up for a moment to stretch my legs and from the porthole caught a glimpse of the view below. Through the clouds the moon cast a magical light over a finger of coastline set in a sea of silver. It was unexpectedly beautiful. I felt a sudden urge to paint it.

But something about the encounter with Major Churchill had unsettled Petr. As I sat down again he addressed a remark to me. The propellers were suddenly throbbing even more noisily than before and he had to speak quite loudly over the sound of the engines. He shouted in my ear, 'Ilic says you're not really a woman.'

'Are you crazy? Of course I'm a woman.'

'I think you're a woman, but Ilic wants you to prove it.'

'Don't be insulting, comrade.'

Occasionally one of the partisans in our unit, fired up with *rakija,* would suggest that I might join him in a recreational bout of sexual intercourse, but I was forbidding and physically strong enough to repel their advances. In the end they respected me too much to force the issue. But I was under no illusions: had they pushed their luck and in their excitement got to the point of discovering my ultimate maleness, they would probably have shot me in the head. And then shot themselves in the head too.

There was something unusually menacing about my two comrades tonight. I realised that they too had been drinking steadily throughout the flight. They were either side of me now, unpleasantly persistent. 'Just show us what you've got in there, why don't you?' Ilic was grappling with my belt.

'What are you, perverts? You dream that I have a *kurac* because that would excite you? You want your women to be men? You have degraded tastes, comrades.'

But Ilic's hands were tugging remorselessly at my trousers, and Petr was pinioning my arms. Perhaps it had started as a joke, but it was no longer funny. I was frightened. There was a terrible symmetry between the exposure of my manhood and my exposure as a spy for British Intelligence. Neither revelation must be allowed to happen.

The aircraft was coming in to land. The engines thundered louder than ever. Part of my mind registered that something was wrong with the plane, that it was struggling, wallowing like a ship in a heavy sea. But I was simultaneously occupied in repelling the attacks of my two inflamed comrades. There was a succession of sudden bucks and lurches which threw several passengers from one side of the cabin to the other. The last thing I remember was kicking out as Ilic exploited the chaos to get his hand inside my trousers. He had just grabbed hold of my manhood and was cursing in fury and outrage when the most God Almighty explosion threw us all upwards as the Dakota hit the ground and broke up.

Perhaps it was my circus training that saved me, an instinctive motion of my body that guided me in my fall. As I lay dazed on the rocky ground of the airfield watching the transport plane in flames, my first thought was to refasten my trousers. It was then that I realized I had sprained my wrist. Thankfully that was my only injury. Petr and Ilic, on the other hand, were killed outright. Air Commodore Carter was fatally injured and died the next day. Waugh and Randolph Churchill sustained minor (but I hope quite painful) burns.

I saw Churchill in the first aid station. He was weeping maudlin, drunken tears. It appeared his batman had been killed. As I was led away to get my wrist bandaged up, I was conscious of Waugh's eyes following me. I heard him drawling, 'Cheer up, Randolph. You may have lost your servant, but at least your pretty little Jug's in one piece.'

I read through all of Waugh's diaries for that summer of 1944. In idle moments on Vis he apparently enjoyed bandying to anyone who'd listen the theory that Marshal Tito was actually a woman. This did little to foster good relations with the Partisans, may indeed have consolidated Belgrade's post-war alignment with Moscow rather than Washington or London. I sometimes wonder if, subliminally, I was responsible for Waugh's flight of fancy about Tito. Did the breath of my own transvestite state waft up to him along the length of that Dakota?

After the war I did two things. I became a full-time woman, and I became a full-time landscape painter. I was quite successful at both. My increasingly admired views of the Aegean and Dalmatian coast were now signed Adriana Lush. I had a series of sell-out exhibitions at the Fine Art Society in London in the 1950s and 1960s.

I also published my own autobiography in 1963, which I called *Crossing Over.* I got a little carried away and included an over-imaginative account of an amorous liaison I said I'd had with Randolph Churchill on war service in Dalmatia. As result of the ensuing legal action the entire edition of the book was pulped. Strange that, isn't it? If you're Evelyn Waugh, you can question the gender of Marshal Tito in print and get away with it. But if you're Adriana Lush, you're allowed no such satirical headroom.

# Sublimation
## Vienna,1912

*Look how fast the telegraph poles go by. It's like they're chasing each other.*

*But they never catch each other, do they, Gerti?*

*Are we nearly there yet? I'm bored.*

*Only another hour. This train's an express.*

*What are you doing?*

*Drawing you, Gerti.*

*I'm not taking my dress off in the train.*

*I'm not asking you to take your dress off. I'm just drawing you sitting there, counting the telegraph poles.*

Please lie down on this couch.
Why?
It makes it easier for us to talk freely, Herr Schiele.
But I can't see you, Herr Doktor Freud.

I am here, just around the corner. You will talk more freely if you can't see me.

But how are you going to hypnotise me? That's what you do, isn't it?

No. I just want you talk to me, to tell me what is troubling you.

Anyone would be troubled if they had suffered what I have suffered.

Tell me what happened to you.

I was held in a cell, Herr Doktor. I was incarcerated. For twenty-four days I was under arrest. You know how many hours that is? Five hundred and seventy-six! An eternity!

Of what were you accused, Herr Schiele?

Of being an artist.

I am not aware that this is a criminal offence. Or not yet, even in Vienna.

I tell you I would not have been accused in court if I had not been an artist. I was on trial because of some drawings I made, drawings that the judge said were corrupting.

What sort of drawings were they?

Drawings of the human body. Where is the shame in that? And yet there was this judge sitting there in the district court who thought differently. No doubt he fancied himself as a man of cultural discernment, someone who has visited churches, museums, theatres, concerts, and yes probably even art exhibitions. A man who consequently is numbered among the educated class which has read or at least heard of the way artists live and work. And yet this man permitted me to be locked up in a cage! Hindering the artist is a crime. It is murdering life in the bud. It is a crime far worse than anything I was accused of. I was in the dock just because I was doing my work as an artist. Because I draw pictures of the human body.

Drawings of genitals?

Naturally. I must be honest as an artist. I must tell the truth. Sex is very important to human beings.

It is all-important, Herr Schiele. The deepest essence of human nature consists of instinctual impulses, which are of an elementary nature, which are similar in all men and which aim at the satisfaction of certain primal needs.

Sexual needs.

That is so. The sex instinct is at the root of everything we do, including making art. Let us talk a little more about your art, about the making of pictures. Do you understand what I mean by Sublimation?

Sublimation? No-one could sublimate the misery I have been through. I have had to bear unspeakable things.

I don't deny that you have. But I am speaking of something different, something that is a most important process to the artist. It is what helps him to create art.

What do you know about art?

Not as much as you. But I have observed the ways of artists.

And that gives you the right to criticise me?

I am not criticising you. I want to help you. I want to help you understand yourself, and what it is that you do when you make pictures.

You are just the same as that judge in St Polten, the one who dared to sit in judgement on me. You know what he did? He sat there in his robes at the trial and he took one of the confiscated drawings, and he held it up in his hand. It was the one that had hung in my bedroom, the one that he said had corrupted children because I had allowed them to see it. Then he set fire to it. He solemnly burned it over a candle flame! *Auto da fé*! Inquisition! Middle Ages! Castration, Hypocrisy! Go then to the museums and cut up the greatest works of art into little pieces. He who denies sex is a filthy person who smears in the lowest way his own parents who have begotten him.

Herr Schiele, I have already told you I am certainly not denying the sexual instinct – I acknowledge it as the one that gives energy to all our actions.

So what is this sublimation?

Sublimation enables excessively strong excitations arising from particular sources of sexuality to find an outlet and use in other fields. It's one of the origins of artistic activity.

I am an artist. I am in touch with my instinct. If I am not in touch with my instinct I am not an artist. If I am not a sexual being I am not an artist.

Then we both agree on the power and importance of human instinct. But the greatest art is created when the artist deploys the sublimation of the excitations produced by his sexual instinct. If these excitations are rechannelled into art they create an even greater energy, an even greater fertility of the imagination. And an even greater work of art.

So, Herr Doktor, you are telling me that every drop of sperm spilt is a masterpiece lost?

No, that's not what I am saying. Sexual gratification is essential to the human being. Repression of that instinct is dangerous, it's one of the prime causes of neurosis. But there is another way of dealing with excessive sexual energy, one that avoids repression. This involves its rechannelling in order to produce art.

Yes, but what you are saying is that if a man is totally sexually satisfied, he cannot produce art.

It is not in the nature of man to be continuously sexually satisfied. Thus art arises. To paraphrase Horace: *Ars longa, coitus brevis.*

You can talk in your Latin, but you are no better than the art critics. They understand nothing about what it is to be an artist. What it is to make a work of art.

What do they not understand?

They go at it all wrong. An art critic who analyses a picture is like a man who during coition suddenly comes up with observations about love.

I don't claim to be an art expert, Herr Schiele, but last year I wrote a psychological study of Leonardo da Vinci. It became clear to me that we can best account for Leonardo's extraordinary artistic and scientific achievements in terms of his sublimated sexuality, specifically his homosexuality.

Homosexuals? Those people are perverts.

You are a married man, Herr Schiele?

No. But I love women, not men.

When did you first have sexual feelings?

I was a child. Have adults forgotten how they themselves as children were incited and aroused by the impulse of sex? Have they forgotten how terrible passion burned in them and tormented them when they were still children? I have not forgotten, for I suffered terribly from it.

You have sisters?

I didn't have sex with my sister.

It doesn't matter if you did.

Gerti is a very beautiful girl.

I am sure she is.

I took her there because we both wanted to go. It may even have been her idea.

Where did you take her?

To Trieste, on the train. When my father died. We still had his railway pass, but it was due to expire at the end of the month.

Why did you go to Trieste?

Because it's where my father took my mother on their honeymoon.

And tell me, how old were you when you went with Gerti to Trieste?

I was sixteen and she was twelve.

How long did you stay there?

Just one night. We took a room in the same hotel where our parents had stayed.

*Don't move, Gerti. Stay still, exactly as you are. Looking out of the window.*

*Why don't I just take my dress off now we're in the hotel?*

*No, it's got to be like that, half hanging from your hips. It's how I want to draw you.*

*But it's in the way, it's uncomfortable.*

*Don't think about it. Think about something else. Tell me what you can see out of the window.*

*I can see boats, fishing boats. Bobbing in the harbour. Coloured fishing boats, painted red and blue, tied up to the quay. Will you be done soon?*

*Only another few minutes.*

*I'm hungry.*

*Just let me finish this drawing. Then we're going to go out to the restaurant.*

*Is it a big restaurant? With Schnitzel? And ices?*

*If you like.*

*What's this town called again?*

*Trieste.*

*And they speak Italian here, don't they?*

*A lot of them do.*

*I don't like Italians.*

*Why not?*

*They look at me in a funny way.*

*They look at me in a funny way, too.*

*Yes, but that's different. They look at you because you're from Vienna. But they look at me because I'm a girl.*

Did you have sex with her?

No I told you, Herr Doktor, I did not.

But you had sexual feelings for her?

No. I was too busy drawing her.

Ah, Herr Schiele, that's exactly my point. That's sublimation.

# Shipboard Romance

## One

Valerie Walter walked slowly into the club library and sank into the chair best positioned to take advantage of the gentle breeze generated by a large slowly-turning fan in the ceiling above. She arranged her thin, stylishly-cut dress about her long, elegant legs. God, Ceylon was hot. No-one had told her that Colombo in February was going to be quite as sweltering as this. She looked about her. She seemed to be alone, apart from three elderly members out on the verandah who were lying on wicker daybeds sleeping off their lunch, bandana handkerchiefs spread over their perspiring foreheads. She summoned the native servant to bring her another glass of lemonade, then took up the two-day old copy of *The Times* of London and turned to the sports page.

England, she read, had made 341 in their first innings of the Fourth Test against Australia at Adelaide. Colin Cowdrey had contributed 79 of them. There was a grainy photograph of

Cowdrey's generously proportioned form despatching the ball to the boundary. She peered at it forensically. No. Not a glimmer of a chance that this was the man she was looking for. She crossed him off her list of possibles. She could add his name to those of Len Hutton, Peter May, Tom Graveney, Frank Tyson and Godfrey Evans as identified and accounted for. That left eleven remaining.

A voice at her shoulder said, 'Forgive my asking, but are you a cricket *aficionado*? I have noticed you often studying the test match reports.'

She looked up and saw that a very smartly dressed Ceylonese was addressing her. She noticed the immaculacy of his starched collar, the straightness of his tie, and the silk handkerchief flowering from the breast pocket of his blazer. What had Angus told her? 'They've let in one or two natives as members. Had no choice, really, what with Independence and all that. Only the better types, of course, and by and large they're decent chaps.'

She said she was interested in the scores from Australia. England were doing rather well, weren't they?

'Very much so,' said her new friend. 'I too am following the progress of the test matches each day.'

'I like to see the photographs of the games,' she added casually. She had to be careful not to give herself away. 'The trouble is that the images are so unclear. You can't always make out the players' faces, can you?'

'That's because they are sent by wireless. These are the marvels of modern science: Hutton hits a four and hours later a photo of the stroke is printed in a newspaper the other side of the world. But you are right, the definition often leaves something to be desired.'

'Such a pity,' she said vaguely, not sure where this conversation was leading; not sure where she wanted it to go.

There was a brief silence while he picked up a book, inspected it and laid it down again. Then he said, 'If you wish to see better photographs of the English cricketers, I could show you my collection.'

'You have a collection? How marvellous.'

'I have been assembling it over the past year. A photographic record of all the current test players. Not just those of India and England and Australia, but New Zealand and South Africa and even the West Indies. Would you be interested to see it?'

'That's extremely kind of you, Mr... er...'

'Lakshan de Silva at your service, Madam.' He paused, perhaps sensing the need to emphasise the legitimacy of his presence in the club. 'You probably know my family firm? De Silva Transport. It is the second biggest shipping concern in Ceylon.'

'Ah, yes, I think I've heard of it,' she lied. 'And I would very much like to see your scrap book, of the English players particularly.'

'Not so much a scrap book. More an archive, you know.'

'Ah, yes indeed. Of course. An archive. Tell me, do you... do you have photos of all the players who are touring Australia at the moment? The whole party?'

'Naturally, I have all seventeen of them. I will bring them in tomorrow. It would be a pleasure to be of service to such a lovely young lady, particularly one who shares my passion for cricket. Shall we say around 6.30 if that is convenient? You will be here then?'

'I will make sure I am. Thank you, Mr de Silva.'

Angus was inclined to be difficult about driving all the way in to the club again next day, but in the end she got her way by telling him that the Mackesons were going to be dining so there would definitely be bridge afterwards. She had no idea if this was true, but sometimes you had to be creative in order to get what you wanted. She had only been married to Angus for six months, and had only been living in Ceylon for four, but she was a quick learner.

Mr de Silva was waiting for her in the library. 'I hope this file will be of interest. As you requested, it contains the photographs of all the English players currently on tour in Australia.'

'Thank you so much,' she said, and began the process of identification that would settle her uncertainty once and for all. She brought out of her handbag her own list of the names, to check them off. She needed to see photographs of each of the remaining players: Edrich, Simpson, Wilson, Bedser, Statham, Bailey, Appleyard, Loader, Wardle, McConnon, and Andrew. She found Edrich first. Definitely not. He was the one who was almost bald and looked about a hundred. Then Bedser was the one who resembled a rather somnolent bear: it certainly wasn't him. Wilson was a nonentity who struck no chord of memory, ditto Statham, Bailey, Appleyard, Andrew and Wardle. McConnon and Loader looked distinctly spivvy types – she remembered them now, joshing in the swimming pool - and could similarly be rejected. That appeared to be all. No, wait a minute: one player's photograph was missing. She double-checked the omission on her own list of names.

'Mr de Silva, look, there doesn't seem to be one of R.T. Simpson.'

Mr de Silva sorted swiftly through the postcard-size images. 'Let me see. No, you are correct. This photograph must have slipped out. That is most upsetting. It must be in another file.'

But Val instinctively knew that she'd found her man, by a process of elimination. It must be R.T. Simpson. He was the only one left.

'Tell me about Simpson,' she asked. 'Is he an amateur or a professional?' It suddenly seemed rather important.

'R. T. Simpson is the captain of Nottinghamshire. He is an amateur.'

It was ridiculous, but she actually felt a murmur of relief at the news. 'Does R. T. Simpson have a nickname, do you know? To his team-mates, I mean? Could it be 'Des'?'

"Des'?' Mr de Silva repeated with a perplexed expression, as if enunciating an unfamiliar technical term. 'I am not informed on this matter.'

As far as Val was concerned, however, the question was settled. Reginald Thomas Simpson was Des. He must be, because all the other candidates had been crossed off her list, and he was the only one left. Her quest was at an end. She had finally pinned down the man she was seeking, the guilty party.

She cast her mind back to the beginning of the story. To her own age of innocence.

## Two

Four and a half months earlier, on 15 September 1954, the newly married Mrs Valerie Walter had embarked with her husband Angus on the *Orsova* at Tilbury. The liner was bound for Perth, Australia; she and Angus were only going as far as Colombo, but it would take two weeks, and she was looking forward to the voyage like billy-oh. She was twenty-four, and she was determined to enjoy herself, to make the most of her new marital status. What had her Aunt Josephine told her? Look, Val, she'd opined, gin in one hand and a cigarette in the other, people say the post-war world's changed but it hasn't in one respect. You can still have a lot more fun as a married woman than as a single one. You have more latitude, if you know what I mean. Just be careful. And discreet. Her mother's message to her on the night before her wedding had been rather more conventional, more restrained. And more restraining. Your first duty is towards your husband, she'd said. Angus is a good man, so love him and look after him. Always put him number one in your life and you won't go far wrong. Frankly, Val preferred her aunt Josephine's prescription. *Liberté, Chérie*, murmured Josephine in her ear. Josephine had spent the years since the war in France, partying between Paris and the *Côte d'Azur*. OK, she had got through two husbands in the process. But she'd lived life on her own terms. And anyway, why couldn't you have it both ways?

Look after your husband, of course, but also have a good time. Take advantage of the opportunities that your married status opened up for you.

The moment she stepped on board Val felt she'd entered a kind of floating paradise. Every aspect of the ship that was to be the field of her operations and the source of her pleasures for the next fortnight was fascinating to her. Its sheer size took her breath away: the spaciousness of its different decks, the splendour of its cabins, and the luxury of their fitments; the grandeur of the first-class bars and dining rooms, the assiduous attentions of the staff, and the never-ending drinks and jollity. The accoutrements of the deck had their own romance, too, the funnels and vents and rails and winches, the ropes and tarpaulins and the lifeboats and the cables and the hoists and the scuppers and the spars. How clean the wooden surface of the decks looked, and how regularly and meticulously the crew washed them down. And she liked the way from the comfort of her bed she could sometimes hear the ship's bell sounding, marking out the watches of the night.

'What do you know about cricket, my angel?' said Angus that first evening as they sat down together at their table in the dining room.

She had noticed that since she had become married to him, as opposed to courted by him, Angus's attempts at conversation had grown increasingly ponderous. 'Cricket? Not a lot. Why do you ask?'

'Because for the next two weeks you're going to be sharing this voyage with the England cricket team.'

'Really, darling?'

'Yup. They're on their way to Australia to play a series of test matches. And they're travelling with us on this ship.'

She didn't give much further thought to it that first evening. But gradually, as the huge liner cut a mercifully untroubled passage through the swell of the Bay of Biscay, as the rays of the autumn sun strengthened, she began to spot them, wandering the decks. They wore smart blazers and open-necked shirts and looked bronzed and healthy, and somehow bigger than most of the other passengers. Sometimes they shed their blazers and played vigorous games of deck quoits or tennis. Sometimes they shed more of their clothing and went swimming in the pool, where their muscled bodies were a guilty pleasure to run her eyes over. In the evenings some of them wore dinner jackets.

'Why don't they all wear dinner jackets?' she asked Angus on the second night.

'Because some of them are professionals. It's mostly the amateurs who dress for dinner. Look, there's Peter May. He's wearing one, of course.'

Peter May had a distant, slightly anxious expression on his face. 'Is he the captain?'

'No,' said Angus. 'The captain's Len Hutton. Look, over there.'

She followed his gaze to a wiry man with a gnarled, lived-in face. He didn't look entirely at ease in his dinner jacket, as if he had been forced into it and was now trapped by it, constricted by its unfamiliarity. 'So he'd be an amateur, of course. As captain.'

A troubled expression crossed Angus's face. 'Well, no. As it happens he's… he's a professional.'

'The captain's a professional?'

Angus sighed. It was a sigh that spoke of a sad and imperfect world, a place where dangerous change was in the air. 'That's it, I'm afraid. He's the first professional player to captain England.'

'If he's a professional and he's been made captain, then surely they wouldn't have chosen him unless he's the best cricketer in England. And in that case he should be captain.'

'Well, yes and no, my sweet. He may be the best cricketer in England but that doesn't that make him the best captain.'

'Why not?'

The pained expression returned to Angus's face, the one she recognised he always adopted when forced to confront something that undermined the certainties of life. 'To be a good captain you have to be a natural leader of men. That's something that amateurs are generally better at.'

'Times are changing, and a darned good thing.'

She didn't really believe what she was saying but sometimes she enjoyed getting a rise out of Angus. He paused, then reached out his hand across the table and squeezed hers. 'Of course you can say that kind of thing to me, in private, because we're man and wife,' he went on, 'but please don't talk like that when we get to Colombo. It would upset people.'

'Who would it upset?'

'The chaps at the club. There are some very good fellows there.'

'Of course I won't let you down, Angus, in your precious club. I'm really not the dangerous socialist you imagine, you know.'

'No, of course you aren't darling.' She realised then what it was that she found most irritating about her husband. It was the patronising tone in his voice.

During the silence that followed, something rather more exciting than the pros and cons of Len Hutton's right to wear a dinner jacket caught her attention. In amongst the bunch of players congregated at the bar prior to taking their places at the dinner table was a man who kept looking in her direction. Eyeing her. A woman knows, she thought to herself. It made her feel uneasy, self-conscious that this unknown cricketer was looking at her in that way; but underneath a little breathless excitement fluttered. Really, Val, she told herself, you shouldn't be having these thoughts. You've only been married two months.

In the following days she sighted him twice more in. Once he was walking away from the bar with drinks in his hand just as she came in, and he looked back over his shoulder very deliberately to inspect her. And then another morning as she was strolling with Angus across the promenade deck he passed them by and caught her eye. She would not forget that moment. It was over before she had registered it, but very discreetly, very charmingly he had winked at her. Ah, the sweet complicity of that wink. She built a whole edifice of dreams on it.

As they cruised across the Mediterranean towards Naples the sea and the skies got bluer and the sun got warmer and the jollity ratcheted up several notches. People drank more; the draw for the deck quoits competition generated a succession of keenly contested matches and a gathering amount of acrimony; there was an increase in the volume of the splashing and shrieking in the swimming pool; and plans were laid for a gala fancy-dress party. The dancing after dinner now lasted into the small hours.

Angus was not a very keen dancer. He preferred to settle down to some serious bridge after dinner. He'd found a chap called Mackeson, also a tea planter, who had a wife and an unmarried sister in tow. The Mackesons were delighted for Angus to make up a four with them. 'You don't mind, darling, do you?' he asked her each evening. 'Of course not, darling,' she said.

So Val left him to it and spent more time in the ball room. There was no shortage of partners for her there. She rather enjoyed the way men queued up to dance with her. She danced with them all, from the ship's doctor to the middle-aged Colonel on his way to a posting in Port Said, to the taciturn Australian accountant who was nonetheless an unexpectedly elegant mover. But she never danced with any of them more than once of an evening. She had her reputation to preserve. Always discreet, Aunt Josephine had told her. Stay a little bit unattainable. It'll only make you more desirable. In between times she wandered the decks, enjoying the warmth of the night and the spectacle of the silver moon over the sea.

One thing perplexed and frustrated her. Her cricketing admirer didn't seem to frequent the dance floor. She often looked around for him amongst the throng of excited dancers, or on the fringes contemplating entering the fray. She had it planned. How across the ballroom she would catch his eye and smile at him, returning his wink as it were, communicating her availability for the next dance. But he was never there. It wasn't as if some training-regime edict had gone out that the touring party were not to dance, because quite a few of the players were enthusiastic participants. There was Tom Graveney, who was a batsman, apparently, and a bit of a stylist. There was Godfrey Evans, who was the wicket keeper and deftly light on his feet. There was a balding terrier of a man called Frank Tyson who was said to be a demon of a fast bowler, and looked as though given half the chance he would sink his teeth into the human prey he was propelling so vigorously round the dance floor. But infuriatingly her admirer didn't deign to put in an appearance.

The night before docking in Colombo the dancing was particularly wild. The combination of the drink and the music and the moonlit tropical night infected the revellers with a kind of Dionysian frenzy that was intensified by an awareness that arrival in Ceylon tomorrow heralded the final leg of the journey, and all human pleasures must come to an end. But not tonight. She danced with the purser this time, and the Australian accountant. Then, suddenly, he was at her shoulder. Her cricketer. 'May I have the pleasure of this one?' he said. He was very polite and formal. He danced well. His arm felt very strong around her back. When the music paused he asked her if he could have the next one, too, and she relaxed her principles instantly. 'I don't see why not,' she breathed.

Later they went out to get some air. They stood at the rail looking out at the moonlight across the water. He said, 'You know you're the most beautiful woman on board this ship.'

'Am I?' she said.

An odd thing had happened. Without any consciousness of the manoeuvre, she found they had both edged a little further into the lee of a lifeboat, so that they were hidden from the view of casual passers-by. And all at once he was kissing her on the lips.

A little later he said, 'We could go back to my cabin.'

'Could we?' she giggled. She'd had too much champagne, of course she had, but it would have been ridiculous not to have that third glass on a night like this.

'I think it might be rather enjoyable if we did.'

'What about my husband?'

'He's having a great time at the bar. No need to disturb him.'

'You're one of the cricketers, aren't you?' she murmured as she ran her fingers through his gently Brylcreamed hair. 'The England cricketers.'

'I might be.'

'What's your name?'

'You can call me Des. It's what my special friends know me as.'

Now he seemed to have his tongue in her ear. It was rather nice. She didn't want it to stop. So she went with him to his cabin. Here at some unquantifiable point on the ocean between Aden and Ceylon she wasn't really anywhere. Whatever happened now didn't count.

'Don't worry, sweety,' he breathed through the Brylcream. 'I'll pull out in time. The newspapers say my timing's impeccable.'

After it was over, she got dressed again, smoothed down her hair, and let herself out of the cabin door. Glancing back at the bed she saw that Des seemed to have fallen asleep. Thank

God, there was no-one about in the corridor. It all felt curiously unreal, as though she was acting in a film, as though this whole sequence of events was only unfolding in celluloid. When she regained her own quarters she found Angus wasn't back yet. Only then did the routine actions that she began to perform gradually reconnect her with real life: washing her face, cleaning her teeth, brushing out her hair; undressing, and pulling on her nightdress. As she slipped into bed, she was disconcerted to catch a quick whiff of Brylcream. She banished it with a dash of her own scent behind each ear.

Angus came in quarter of an hour later very definitely the worse for wear. He'd had several gin fizzes and a couple of rubbers of bridge. 'What did you get up to, my angel?' he slurred.

'Oh, I had one or two dances then I turned in.'

It had been the strangest night of her life. She had done things of which she had not suspected herself capable. On balance she had rather enjoyed it.

Angus and she disembarked for good the following morning at Colombo. The England players disembarked too, but only for a day. They were due to play a game against a Ceylonese side, and there was considerable local excitement in the town.

'Why don't we stay and watch?' she suggested to Angus.

'No,' said Angus. 'We've got to get up to the estate. They're expecting us.'

She felt frustrated. At the very least she'd like to see Des playing. From a distance, of course. She wasn't going to get all sentimental about him, that wasn't what drove her. She was just curious about him, to see how good he was with a bat or a ball in his hand. 'That bloody plantation. I suppose this is it, is it? I'm going to be holed up in that bloody place for the rest of my life.'

The infuriating thing about Angus was the way he never lost his temper. The way what he said and did was always informed by the sweetest of reason. 'Of course not, my angel,' he said. 'It's less than an hour's drive away, except in the rainy season. We'll come back into town two or three nights a week, I promise, and dine in the Club.'

'What's the Club like?'

'You'll love it. Lots of nice people are members. There's a really good bridge competition, too. Very high standard.'

'You know I don't like bridge.'

'This will be the chance for you to take some lessons. We'll have you up to tournament standard in no time at all.'

'Is there dancing?'

'Some evenings, of course there is.'

It was in the jeep as they were driven up to the plantation that afternoon that the thought she had been suppressing finally burst through into her consciousness: what if she was pregnant? What if Des was the father? Des, who was on his way to Australia to play cricket for several months. Des, whose proper name she had never actually discovered. She went through the list of players in her mind. She could put faces to some of their names: Hutton, May, Graveney, Evans and Tyson. But what of the others? Which one of them had the nickname Des? Which one of them was potentially the father of her child? She needed to see photographs of the entire team in order to pick him out. She wouldn't forget his face, she'd recognise it when she saw it again. The man whose cabin she had so memorably visited with such sensual consequences had had a thick and lustrous head of hair, warm brown eyes, a cleft in his chin, and nostrils that flared when he was excited.

Just before Christmas she went to see Doctor Macpherson, the Scottish physician with a practice in a spacious white bungalow two leafy streets away from the club. He had presided over the health of the European community longer than most people could remember. There was a leaden inevitability to the news he gave her, although he seemed to be disproportionately excited about it. He spoke of 'a happy event', and told her how lucky she was. How long have you been married? Six months, she told him. There you are, he said triumphantly, as if he had personally conjured the miracle of conception. Out in the tropics some English women took six years of trying before they achieved her happy condition, he told her. Some never managed. It was to do with the climate. The humidity. It wasn't always conducive to marital relations. He patted her arm in a gesture of benign congratulation.

## Three

As she came into the club three days after her first encounter with Mr de Silva she was handed an envelope that had been left for her at the reception desk. It contained a letter from him, and a photograph. Here was the missing portrait of Reginald

Thomas Simpson. She stared at it, bemused. It wasn't what she expected at all. It showed a man with crinkly dark hair. He was not bad looking. But he was most emphatically not Des. Not under any circumstances.

In her perplexity she took up Mr de Silva's letter.

*Dear Mrs Walter,*

*First, many congratulations to you on your country's famous victory over Australia in the Fourth Test. You must be very pleased that England have retained the Ashes.*

*Second, many apologies for the mislaying of the photograph of R.T. Simpson which I located in the wrong file and am sending to you now. You also asked me a further question when we last met. I have checked through the many reference books, published interviews and press articles that I have to hand, and there is no record anywhere of either R.T. Simpson or any member of the England cricket team having the nickname 'Des'. I hope this information is of use to you.*

*I remain, dear Mrs Walter, your most faithful servant*

*L. de Silva.*

It took her a moment to assimilate that the man who had made hot love to her in that steamy cabin was no more a member of the England cricket team than Angus. So it gradually dawned on her: Des had been some kind of confidence trickster, a hanger-on to the England party, passing himself off as one of them when in actual fact he was just another passenger. She'd been had, in more ways than one.

'Shall we have a gin fizz before dinner, darling?' It was Angus talking to her.

'Good idea,' she said.

He guided her through to the club bar. 'Are you feeling OK? Not too sick? We've got to look after you now. What with the little one on board.'

'I'm feeling absolutely fine, Angus. Don't fuss.'

'What have you got there in that envelope?'

'Oh, it's just a photograph of one of the England players. Mr de Silva has got it into his head that I share his interest in cricket and pretty much forced it on me.'

'Let me see. Ah, R.T. Simpson, captain of Nottinghamshire. Are you sure you don't have a bit of a thing for him?'

'So you've found me out. R.T. Simpson and I made passionate love all through the voyage,' she laughed. She intended her laugh to be captivating. 'You are ridiculous, Angus, do you know that?'

She was in fine form over dinner. Now she knew the truth about Des an absolute conviction gripped her. Of course the baby was Angus's. How many times had he made love to her since their wedding? At least fifty, she calculated. What her husband lacked in imagination as a lover he made up for in the regularity and diligence of his performance. How many times had she been to bed with Des? Just once. One solitary occasion. She really shouldn't worry. The odds were stacked against Des being the father. And anyway he'd promised to pull out, hadn't he, even if the newspaper reports on the impeccability of his timing had been no more than his own fabrication. It would all be smoothed over, worn away and forgotten in the passage of time. But now she came to think of it, England cricketer or not, he had been rather marvellous.

'Darling,' she said, as the plates were cleared away and she lifted her third gin fizz to her lips. 'I've been thinking. Maybe the time has come.'

'For what, my sweet?'

'Well, over the next few months I should probably take things a bit easier. I'll have a bit more time on my hands. Maybe I should start those bridge lessons.'

Angus looked up at her. His eyes were shining with pleasure and gratitude, if possible even more pleasure and gratitude than he had shown three weeks ago when she had told him that there was a baby on the way.

What had Aunt Josephine said to her? 'Make the most of the voyage, my darling,' she had counselled, drawing deep on her cigarette. 'Exciting places, liners. And remember: what happens at sea stays at sea.'

# Giving Something Back

## One

'I'll be frank with you, Derek. This may sound arrogant, but I don't need the money anymore. I've got more than enough to see me through the rest of my life in comfort. Even with all that bloody alimony I pay. Lost the thrill of the chase, I suppose. Making moulah just doesn't do it for me like it used to. I need a new stimulus. I've mulled it over, and I think what you're proposing might just give me that. You've come to me at the right moment.'

'You don't have to do it, you know. I don't want you to feel pressurised.'

'No, I've thought about it. I'm up for it. If it's in the national interest. Patriotic duty and all that. Not to mention helping out an old mate.'

'I still need you to think about it one more time, Alastair. Pull out now, and there'll be no hard feelings. Our conversations never took place, we forget all about it. But after today, if you do choose to go ahead, then you're committed. Committed to doing things our way, even if our interests and yours are in conflict. Are you OK with that?'

'The way I look at it, my country's been pretty good to me. I'm not saying I've always agreed with the precise political complexion of the government of the day, but overall it's given me the freedom to prosper. It's my home, it's my heritage. So. Time I gave something back.'

'We're on then, are we?

'Good to go.'

'In that case I'll need you to put your signature to this. Take a few moments to read it through.'

'Ah, right. The Official Secrets Act. That looks very grown-up.'

'Make sure you understand it. Any questions, ask now, not later. It's important that you're sure.'

'Funny, though, isn't it?'

'What's funny?'

'Forty years on, for you and me to be having this conversation. Couldn't have imagined it when we were at Cambridge.'

'A lot of water under the bridge since Cambridge. Keep reading.'

'Unlike you I can read and talk at the same time.'

'Just let me know if you have questions.'

'OK, here's one: did you ever have second thoughts? About your career, I mean?'

'I think I always knew I had a Foreign Office cast of mind.'

'So no regrets.'

'No regrets. And you?'

'Plenty of regrets. But no remorse. I always knew I wanted to make a bit of cash. The art market seemed a less uncivilised way of doing it than the City. Here you are. Signed and sealed.'

'Thank you. You keep your copy. This one comes with me for the file.'

'So break it to me gently. What exactly is it you want me to do?'

'He's expecting you on Tuesday?'

'That's right. For lunch again. At his chalet in St Moritz.'

'Just the two of you?'

'It generally is.'

'To talk about his pictures?'

'What he wants to buy. What he might be persuaded to sell. I'm there to advise him. Discreetly.'

'Remarkable.'

'What's remarkable?'

'You're one of the very few people on this planet who has that degree of access to him. The man's probably the biggest arms dealer in the world. And one of the most secretive. Does he trust you?'

'I don't think he necessarily trusts anyone. But he listens to me.'

'Fair enough.'

'So what do you want me to do?'

'It's a very, very simple piece of information that we need you to find out for us. We don't need you to do anything different from normal. Fly there, take the taxi to his house, sit down with him, eat his caviar, drink his champagne, tell him what a wise and discerning collector he is, or whatever it is you say to your best clients on these occasions. Just report back on one thing.'

'And what is that one thing?'

'Is he missing a finger.'

'Missing a finger?'

'That's right. Is he minus a digit.'

'He wasn't the last time I met him.'

'That was what, eighteen months ago?'

'Yes. July before last. On his boat.'

'Sure about that? That he had a full complement then?'

'Pretty sure. I'd have noticed at lunch.'

'Why?'

'We ate lobster.'

'See if there's been any change. Since then.'

'Shouldn't be a problem. What was it, an accident with a firearm?'

'That would have a certain irony, for an arms dealer. We don't know.'

'Why's it important?'

'Sorry. Can't tell you that.'

'Which finger would it be?'

'Can't tell you that either.'

'Because you don't know? Or because I don't need to know?'

'Just find out for us, Alastair. That's all you have to do.'

## Two

'This is very good champagne, Julius.'

'You once told me that pictures look better after champagne. It is therefore in my interests to supply you with the best, in order to raise your valuation of my collection.'

'Either way, your collection just gets better and better. Are you in a buying mood at the moment?'

'Not so much. There is a problem, you see.'

'What is that?'

'No more walls.'

'For a moment there I thought you said no more wars.'

'No more wars, that would be a good thing. No more walls, that is a disaster. I am running out of hanging space.'

'Sorry, Julius, and tell me if I'm talking out of turn. But surely you have a vested interest in the occasional war.'

'There you make a common error, my friend. I don't sell arms to people for them to use them. I sell arms to people so that no-one uses them. Armaments don't cause wars any more than umbrellas cause rain.'

'So you believe in mutual deterrence.'

'That's it, preserving the balance of power. I am a peace-maker, if you like.'

'So you wouldn't sell arms to terrorists?'

'Alastair, what do you take me for?'

'I'm sorry. It's none of my business, of course. Let's go back to the more pressing problem of no more walls. If that's really so, you could always sell something. Create a bit of room.'

'Hard to decide what.'

'Look, even the greatest collectors do a bit of thinning out now and then. Deaccession a B-plus picture in order to replace it with an A. Not that there are many B-pluses left here now.'

'What would you suggest?'

'Let's have a look round. Well, not these two, obviously. Pretty incredible: a top 1911 Picasso and a top 1911 Braque hanging next to each other. Tells you everything you need to know about analytical cubism.'

'What about my other Braque? The one from 1921, in the passage? Come with me and refresh your memory.'

'Ah yes. The still life. Well, it's a good one of course. But with Braque 1921 is a lot less desirable as a date than 1911.'

'So now you're standing in front of it, what do you think?'

'I wonder if I could look at it in the natural light from the window. Would you lift it off the wall for me, Julius? Better you drop it than I do. Right, good. Now turn it round, so I can look at the back. What a wonderful dealer's label: Léonce Rosenberg. You don't see that often, with the original stock number too. Thank you.'

'What could I get for it?'

'I'll give it some thought and come back to you.'

'Very well. Just so long as you remember I'm looking for a totally immoral profit on what I paid. Let's go and eat.'

## Three

'He has all his fingers.'

'You are absolutely sure?'

'I counted them. Four either side as he held a Braque up for me so I could look at the back. And two thumbs at the front when he turned round again with it so we could look at the image. All intact.'

'Excellent.'

'And?'

'And what?'

'Aren't you going to tell me why you needed to know? What difference does it make to anything?'

'My dear fellow. I wish I could. But thank you, thank you anyway. We'll stay in touch.'

*Melvyn got up from his laptop and went into the kitchen to make himself a cup of coffee. Things were running out of control, not heading the way he'd intended at all. It happened sometimes when you were writing fiction: the plot would suddenly take on a will of its own. All this absurd stuff about missing fingers, where had that come from? More to the point, where could it possibly be leading? He could feel one of his headaches coming on.*

*It had seemed a good start, an intriguing premise. Two old Cambridge contemporaries, both clever, both successful, but whose careers have developed differently. Derek is the more serious, more orthodox, more buttoned up. He has risen via the Foreign Office to something fairly senior in the Intelligence Service. Senior, and* still operational. He's experienced in the ways of spies. Alastair, on the other hand, is more entrepreneurial, a successful art dealer, a money-maker, a bit of a maverick. MI6 are investigating Julius Magna, secretive international arms dealer, reputedly a major art collector. They're not getting very far: he covers his tracks well. What about his collection? Could that be an angle into his secrets? The service needs to recruit a friendly art dealer to lead them in there. Informally. A friendly art dealer who has already established access to Magna. After all, international art dealers and spies have quite a lot in common. I know the right man to approach, says Derek. I was at Cambridge with him.

As he spooned instant coffee into the mug and waited for the kettle to boil, Melvyn considered how he had conceived Alastair. Early sixties, vain, charming, cunning, quick-witted; divorced, well-connected. Member of White's? Probably not. Member of 5 Hertford Street? Much more likely. At this point in his life attracted by the idea of a little light espionage on his country's behalf, when it's put to him. Finds it glamorous and exotic, maybe more stimulating than the tired old alchemy of turning art into money. It wasn't totally improbable that such a man would respond positively to a proposal from MI6. Particularly when it was broached by a friend he had known for forty years, kept in touch with, off and on, since Cambridge. A seam of conventional patriotism might lie submerged some way beneath the surface of such a character as Alastair, sufficient to turn him from poacher into gamekeeper, to persuade him to spy on his client for his country. So far so plausible.

But what information? What would MI6 want to know about a secretive arms dealer that they could not find out by other covert *means? Something personal about him. Something only to be gar-nered by being in the same room with him. Something to do with what he had in his house. Or something to do with his personal appearance. And so the whole ridiculous rigmarole about missing fingers had sprung unbidden into his imagination, and on to the screen of his laptop.*

*Shit. The milk was off. He'd just have to drink the coffee black. Outside it had come on to rain again. The February lawn was dispiritingly soggy with moss. And there was the massive branch from the oak tree that had come down in the storm last month, lying reproachfully across the grass, crying out to be cut up for fire-wood. He might just allow himself an illicit pre-lunch cigarette, to keep his morale up.*

*Yes. Well. Alastair would be understandably baffled by the mission to establish whether his client still had all his fingers. So would the reader be, but that wasn't necessarily a bad thing. It intensified the mystery, introduced a quasi-surreal element to the drama. Nothing wrong with destabilising the reader's logic at this stage in the narrative. But what is Derek up to? What aspect of the nation's security has Alastair been instrumental in strengthening by providing this information? That would take some ingenuity to determine convincingly. It had to be established at some point, or all the tension would be dissipated. Unless the fate of the plot was to spiral off into some kind of dotty magic realism? No, that definitely wasn't the direction he wanted it to go.*

## Four

'I'm old enough to remember when people lit cigarettes after sex. Now they just look at their mobiles.'

'You snooze, you lose.'

'I suppose it's a generational thing.'

'Will you stop going on? You don't need to keep reminding me I'm younger than you. What do you want me to do? Alert Age Concern and the Emergency Services every time we make love? Look, I'm 28. You're 62.'

'61, actually.'

'Whatever. Get over it.'

'No, I'm curious. I've just brought you to a peak of sexual pleasure and all you do is reach for that bloody phone.'

'Don't flatter yourself, Alastair. I'm not so transported that I can't read an email.'

'What are you worried you're missing?'

'You've got to keep connected. Ahead of the curve. News is my business, don't forget. Wow! Have you seen this?'

'What?'

'What was the name of that client of yours you went to see last week in Switzerland? That arms dealer?'

'I told you not to talk about it. It was in confidence, just between us.'

'You were boasting. Trying to impress me, weren't you?'

'Seriously, you mustn't mention it to anyone. It's sensitive information.'

'I haven't mentioned it to anyone. Look, I'm a lot more discreet than you are. I'm a journalist, remember? I know how to protect my sources. Anyway, if it was someone called Julius Magna, you've just lost a client.'

'Lost a client? What do you mean?

'He's been found dead.'

'Dead?'

'That's what CNN are reporting.'

'Christ. Let me see.'

'Don't snatch. I thought you preferred lighting post-coital cigarettes to looking at mobiles.'

'Hand it over.'

'No. I'll read it to you: "Local police are investigating the death of financier Julius Magna, 69, at his home in St Moritz, Switzerland this morning. Unconfirmed reports say that his body was discovered by a manservant around 10 am, and that he had been the victim of a firearms accident. Notoriously reclusive, Mr Magna was reputedly one of the richest men in Europe, with widespread business interests across several continents. He leaves an estranged wife, Mariella, and two sons".'

'A firearms accident? Is that what it says?'

'It's a man thing, isn't it? All that playing around with guns.'

'Christ.'

'Are you OK? I mean were you like close to this guy?'

'No, no. Not particularly. It's just a shock. After I'd seen him so recently.'

'Look on the bright side. Maybe his family will ask you to sell his art collection now.'

'I can't believe it. He was fine last Tuesday. Hey, where are you going?'

'Back to the flat. Got an early start in the morning. Have you seen my knickers?'

'I wish you'd stay.'

'Don't go there, Al, don't tie me down, OK? I told you before, I need my freedom. And you need your rest. At your age. Oh, there they are. Down by your ankle.'

*Oh, God. Now an unexplained killing. Magna dead. What could that mean? Yes, it ratchets up the melodrama, reflected Melvyn, keeps the reader on his toes. But why's Magna been killed? It's a worrying thing when the writer has no more idea of the answer to that question than the reader. And what about the older man and the much younger girl in bed together? Where did that spring from? Very dodgy ground. Of course, Alastair requires hinterland. He's divorced, and the body has its needs. But a 61 year old making out with a 28 year old? Doesn't it say more about the sad fantasies of a middle-aged author than about the character he has created?*

*What were the fantasies of this middle-aged author? Time for a bit of honesty here, a dose of self-candour. Wouldn't Melvyn, in his own divorced and disenchanted state, be only too happy to find a spirited but compliant 28 year old in his bed? Was writing this, creating this scene, an implicit admission of inadequacy in his own current amatory arrangements? Mona was considerably more than 28 and compliant wasn't the first word that came to mind to describe her. Mervyn himself, meanwhile, was 56. Had he subconsciously pitched the age of his fictional art dealer at five years more than his own in order to give himself hope?*

*He stared at what he had just written, and his eye snagged on 'I've just brought you to a peak of sexual pleasure'. No. Embarrassing, even as irony. He pressed the delete button and the phrase disappeared into oblivion. He replaced it with 'We've barely finished making love'. It was weak, but it would have to do for the time being. He'd come back to it later.*

## Five

'It was a preliminary test. Straight out of the manual. Of course we didn't need to know if he'd lost a finger. We just needed to try you out, to make sure you had the access you claimed and that you could gather and report a straightforward piece of information. You passed with flying colours.'

'A five-finger exercise?'

'If you like.'

'But… but why did he die? Just after I went to visit him?'

'You tell me.'

'You must know more than you're saying. I mean, you were already talking about a possible firearms accident. Before it happened.'

'Was I? I think I remember it was actually you who brought the idea up, not me. It's all just a coincidence.'

'I don't believe in coincidences.'

'Spare me that old cliché. The last desperate cry of the conspiracy theorist. Much more of life than you think is actually explained by innocent coincidence.'

'What do you want me to do now?'

'Nothing. Go on as normal. Send your condolences or whatever you do when a major client dies. Just keep us discreetly informed if anyone from the Magna family makes contact with you.'

'Understood.'

'And not a word to anyone about our collaboration. No pillow talk to your little journalist friend, OK?'

'How do you know about her?'

'My dear fellow, we are an intelligence service. Give us some credit for doing our job.'

*Did that work? Checking on the number of fingers just being a training exercise, an MI6 ploy to test a new source's capacity to report in accurately? It sounded a bit thin as an explanation. Was the reader meant to believe it? Did Melvyn himself even believe it? Nothing for it but to leave that pending and see where Julius's death took things.*

*Christ, if he were serious about this garden he'd do something about the moss on that lawn. Didn't you have to treat it with something at this time of year? He could check at the Garden Centre. And at the same time why not buy a small chain saw? That would soon sort out the visual distraction of the capsized oak branch.*

## Six

'It's Max Magna. I am the son of Julius.'

'Max. I am so sorry about your father. What a terrible thing.'

'Thank you. It was a shock. But we must all move on. We need to take steps with the art collection. We are putting it into new ownership, a Cayman Islands company. We need an up-to-date valuation. Can you provide it for us?'

'Of course. I have the list, and the pictures are fresh in the memory from my recent visit. Leave it with me.'

'Appreciate it.'

'Are you thinking of sales? Down the line, maybe?'

'No. Not on the agenda.'

'OK, understood.'

'There's one other thing, though.'

'Tell me.'

'A painting's turned up that's not on the inventory. I don't think you've valued it before. Would you be able to have a look at it?'

'With pleasure. Can you tell me what it is?'

'I would prefer not to at this stage. I'd like you to see it before we discuss it.'

'OK. Where is it?'

'It's in the Zurich Freeport. Could you meet me there on Thursday? Say 3p.m.'


## Seven

'Where are you going tomorrow?'

'Got to see a picture in Zurich. Want to come? We could spend a couple of nights in the Baur au Lac. You'd enjoy it, it's a very comfortable hotel.'

'OK, Grandpa.'

*Melvyn caught himself up. Wait a minute, do I really want the girl to accompany Alastair to Switzerland? What does the narrative gain from having her hanging round his hotel room while he checks out this newly discovered painting? They'll have to have sex again, probably. That'll only be a distraction, and very likely an embarrassing one. Christ, this coffee's disgusting without milk. Maybe a walk to the village shop to get some fresh will clear the mind. Except it's still raining. God, winter in the country's depressing.*

*When he sat down at his laptop again Melvyn deleted the words 'OK Grandpa', and substituted 'Another time, Grandpa. Can't, I'm afraid. I'm working on a really big piece for the magazine section and I've got to do this interview.' After he'd inserted this new version Melvyn felt marginally better. Why should Alastair get a gratuitous two nights' shagging in the Baur au Lac? He didn't deserve it. The man was too old for it. He'd probably put his back out.*

## Eight

'Soulless places, these Freeports.'

'I don't spend much time in them.'

'I do. There's a lot of art in freeports. A lot of expensive art.'

'I appreciate your coming today, anyway.'

'Not at all, Max. The least I could do. I still can't believe it about your father. Really gutted for you. It was all a dreadful accident, I take it? Cleaning the gun, or something? Didn't realise it was loaded?'

'Something like that.'

'He was in such great form when I visited him two weeks ago. Hard to believe.'

'They've set the picture up in the private viewing room, through that door. But before we go in I just need you to sign this.'

'What is it?'

'An NDA.'

'I've no problem with a non-disclosure agreement. But I think your father always knew he could rely on my discretion.'

'No question. But we need it for this one picture particularly. It's separate from the main collection.'

'Very well. There you go.'

'Appreciate it. Will you come through now.'

'My God, Max. That's a... that's certainly a surprise.'

'You know the painting?'

'I know of it. But I had no idea your father owned it.'

'Is it a good one? Unlike my father, I know nothing about art.'

'It's one of the greatest Van Goghs in private hands. I mean, it's got everything: scale, colour, passionate brushstroke. It's incredibly strong. And it's a self-portrait. Late 1889, a great date, the year before he committed suicide. Look at his ear. He's painted it still bandaged, after he tried to cut it off.'

'I have a question. What is known of its recent history?'

'To be honest, it's been a bit of a mystery. People in the art world remember it from the late 1980s when it sold for a world record price at Sotheby's. It was bought by a rich Asian then. A few years after that the Asian died. And from then on it went missing. Dropped off the radar. I didn't know where it was. I didn't know anyone else who knew where it was. And there were plenty of people trying to find it. It was clear it was no longer in the Asian's family. The heirs must have sold it sometime in the 1990s, very discreetly. When did your father acquire it?'

'I can't tell you that.'

'But how long have you known he had it?'

'Only since he died. There was a letter for me with the will telling me about it. The lawyers gave it to me last week.'

'Well, of course I entirely understand why you got me to sign that NDA just now. It's a huge rediscovery. Sensational. You're absolutely right to keep careful control of who knows about it.'

'So what's it worth?'

'I need to give it some thought.'

'But your gut reaction?'

'North of a hundred million dollars. Maybe even two hundred.'

## Nine

'So what's up? You sounded a little anxious on the telephone.'

'Not so much anxious, Derek; more a bit confused. Thought I'd better report developments to you as soon as possible.'

'You went to see the son? That go OK?'

'Yes. He wanted to know the value of the art collection.'

'And you gave it to him?'

'I'm working on it. Said I'd get back to him.'

'So what's the problem? What's worrying you?'

'It was Max himself. Something about him.'

'Was he aggressive? Threatening? Hiding something, do you think?'

'No, nothing like that.'

'What then?'

'I only noticed at the end of our meeting. When we shook hands.'

'What?'

'He's missing the index finger on his right hand.'

*Oh, for God's sake. I thought we'd done with the missing finger malarkey. Disposed of it. Why bring that back in now? OK, it creates a momentary frisson of drama. Maybe the reader won't necessarily have seen it coming. But whether it's the father or the son without the digit, it still leaves the same problem of supplying a plausible explanation for the loss further down the line. And where's this Van Gogh leading? Van Gogh... missing ear... Max Magna... missing finger. Your obsession with errant body parts is overcomplicating the plot. Stop it. Think of a way to reel it in again. Forget the fingers. Go with the Van Gogh, the Van Gogh has got legs.*

'How very curious. You're saying Max has lost a finger.'

'I thought it might intrigue you.'

'Why are you laughing?'

'You actually believed me, didn't you?'

'Christ almighty, Alastair.'

'I think that's deuce, don't you?'

'OK, touché. If it gives you pleasure. But can we be serious for a moment? Given recent events, I need to ask you about the art collection. Can you tell me more about it?'

'What exactly do you want to know?'

'Its value. A ballpark figure. Millions? Tens of millions? Hundreds of millions?'

'Well, certainly tens of millions.'

'Which offers an interesting angle on how he does business. Or did business.'

'Meaning what, exactly?'

'Meaning that very valuable works of art are excellent vehicles for moving large amounts of money in transactions that need to be kept secret. Magna sells arms to someone dubious, some state under international sanction, for instance. He doesn't want the buyer's money, or not in a way that could be traceable. Much better he should come into the possession of a very valuable painting. One that could be cashed in at a later date. Or maybe not even cashed in, just used as financial ballast in a future transaction.'

'You make the art market sound like some kind of mobile laundry.'

'Its lack of regulation has unique detergent potential. In unscrupulous hands. What sort of things has Magna got in his inventory? Give me an example. What's the most valuable work?'

'Before I do, can I ask you something? Hypothetically?'

'Go ahead.'

'How would I stand if I passed on to you information covered by an NDA I had signed? Legally, I mean? Could they come after me?'

'Look, we're a secret intelligence service. We protect our sources. There would be nothing to link you to that intelligence. It would hardly be in our interests to divulge your part in how we came by it.'

'I said I'd be glad to help you, and I am. But it also occurs to me I could be shooting myself in the foot by telling you too much. Professionally. If there are sales to be made here, there's no getting away from the fact that I'm first in line to do the deals.'

'Yes, but I thought you said you were a spent force. Not interested in trading any more. First duty to your country and all that.'

'No, that's right. I was just thinking it all through. Getting my bearings here.'

'If it worries you, Al, I can assure you we're not going to stand in the way of your conducting business. Provided that business is legitimate.'

'Legitimate?'

'Provided you're making sales of works that have been acquired legally.'

'But you're suggesting a lot of Magna's collection doesn't fall into that category.'

'If that's the case, you wouldn't want to be handling it anyway, would you?'

'No, of course not. But let me think: Magna's paintings can't all have been acquired with funny money. There are certainly works that he bought publicly over the past ten or fifteen years, at international auction, I mean. So Sotheby's and Christie's would have checked on the source of the funds when they were paid for. They'd be clean.'

'OK. Let's look at specific examples. For instance, you were about to tell me what the most valuable work in the collection is.'

'I'd say it's the 1911 Picasso.'

'What's that worth?'

'$30 million plus. He paid $22 million for it in 2010.'

'Is that clean?'

'He bought it at Christie's. So yes, above board. As I say, auction houses don't accept payment for a purchase without satisfying themselves that the money's come from a legal source.'

'But there must be other works in his collection that don't have a recent public auction history.'

'I need to do more research on them.'

'We'd be interested to know more. Anything big whose acquisition is a bit murky. Keep me posted, won't you.'

'Any news on why Magna died? Was it an accident like they say?'

'I can't tell you.'

'Can't, or won't?'

'Exactly.'

## Ten

'I shouldn't be telling you this, but I could be on the verge of doing something amazing.'

'Uh-huh.'

'Just about the biggest art deal anyone's ever brought off. Ever, in the history of the world.'

'Uh-huh.'

'It's very likely that I may shortly be asked to find a buyer for an unbelievably important picture. Discreetly. Can't tell you who it's by, omertà, total secrecy. If I did I'd have to kill you. But if I play my cards right, I could be on for a disgustingly large commission. Obscene amounts of moulah.'

'Uh-huh.'

'Will you put that bloody phone down and listen to me.'

'I am listening to you. Just got to send this Instagram.'

'You've no idea of the tightrope I'm walking here. It's very, very tricky. Maybe the biggest challenge of my professional life. And just as I was thinking of running down operations a bit, taking it easier.'

'So how much?'

'How much what?'

'How much will you make?'

'A life-changing amount.'

'Go for it, tiger. You know something?'

'What?'

'It turns me on when you talk about money.'

*Melvyn was beginning to conceive a distinct aversion from Alastair. The man was a smooth, self-confident bastard. Why should this ageing art dealer be capable of arousing his much younger girlfriend just by talking about the size of the deal he might or might not be about to do? Why was the fantasy sex-life of the character Melvyn had created so different from the reality of his own experience? Mona, he'd breathed in her ear last night, come upstairs with me and I'll bring you to a peak of sexual pleasure. I'm not in the mood, she'd told him. But I could murder a cup of hot chocolate. It was then that he'd remembered he had no fresh milk. Soon after that she'd gone home.*

*So he'd spent the night alone, struggling with the problem of where Alastair was going next. This Van Gogh was all very well, all very tantalising, but decisions were going to have to be reached now about Alastair's next steps. The fact that he was keeping the existence of the picture in Magna's collection quiet from MI6 – not to mention bragging about it to his lover - meant that he was actively considering the possibility of a deal. The money wasn't just turning his girlfriend on. It was turning him on, too.*

## Eleven

'Welcome to Zurich. Again.'

'Thanks for seeing me so soon, Max. Something's come up. An opportunity you should be aware of, something I couldn't in all conscience keep from you. I didn't want to put it on an email. Better to talk about it in person, keep it between us.'

'Go on.'

'The Van Gogh. I've looked into it. Discreetly. I'm fully aware of my NDA obligations. And the fact that making sales is not on your agenda. But the point is, there are people out there just now who would pay a lot of money for it. People in the Middle East, forming a museum collection. They only want the very best. I could get you a really big price.'

'How much?'

'Three hundred million dollars.'

'You said two hundred last time. What changed?'

'It's a unique opportunity. But it's time-sensitive. Might you be tempted? To sell just that one picture?'

'I'd have to think about it.'

'Of course.'

'A lot of moving parts in all this. I can't give you an answer at once.'

'I understand. But in the meantime I strongly advise you not to talk to anyone else in the art world about this. Once it gets out, you get complications. All sorts of no-hopers trying to attach themselves to the deal, muddying the waters. Pushing up the asking price and pushing down the selling price. The great joy of what I'm proposing is that it would be quick and secure. And clean.'

'Clean?'

'Most definitely clean.'

'How would it work exactly?'

'Very simple. I bring the agent of the buyer to the Zurich freeport. He views the picture. The deal is done. They're quick payers.'

'You'd be rewarded by the buyers, not us?'

'If that's the way you want it.'

'So say you get us 300 million. What are they paying you on top?'

'Max, I'll be totally transparent here: maximum 10 per cent. So asking price 330. Anything the buyers shaved off the price would come out of my commission. You'd still get 300.'

'That's all very well, but no-one agrees a deal like this without doing due diligence. Any buyer would insist on more information about the picture's provenance. How much more information?'

'It's just a question of establishing the ownership sequence which took it from the sale at Sotheby's in 1989 via the Asian's collection into your father's company. They might want a glimpse of the bill of sale by which it came into your father's possession.'

'And if it wasn't a financial transaction?'

'Then some sort of document of transfer detailing the entity from which your father acquired it. Does that exist?'

'Possibly.'

'In my experience these things can generally be sorted out. Lawyer to lawyer.'

*The problem with Alastair is he's a hypocrite. A self-deceiving hypocrite. All that crap about giving something back to his country, not being interested in making money anymore. It's just a façade, a façade that crumbles the moment temptation's put in his way. As he walked* *back from the village shop clutching the milk carton, Melvyn heard Alastair arguing back at him: Yes, but it's a career-crowning deal. The biggest ever. You can't turn your back on an opportunity like that. And on the subject of going back on your resolutions, what about you? You're a bit of a fraud yourself, aren't you? You said you'd never do another thriller again, that it was beneath you, that it was interfering with that major novel you really wanted to write. That was why you bought the house in the country, to concentrate on your novel. Please! And now, just because some commissioning editor from the BBC rings you up, here you are doing a radio thriller again. I mean, radio. Not even TV. What are they paying you? £5,000. Pretty paltry by comparison with the $30 million to be made in the Van Gogh deal.*

*Melvyn let himself back into the house. OK Al, go for it if you must. Follow the money. Live out your dream as a man of action. But two can play at that game: you know what I'm going to do tomorrow? I'm going to buy a chain saw.*

## Twelve

'Don't go rogue on us, Al.'

'I don't know what you're talking about.'

'You bloody well do. This clandestine cosying up to Max Magna. Trying to do a deal on a painting by Van Gogh you deliberately kept from us. We don't like being messed around.'

'No, you've got it wrong. I was just probing him a bit. Information gathering. I was going to pass it all on to you.'

'Forgive me if I don't immediately interpret this as an act of individual patriotic initiative. We've been tapping you on your visits to Zurich. We have a record of your conversation with Magna junior in the bar of the Baur au Lac. What you're planning with these people is a serious criminal offence. We now have incontrovertible evidence that the Magna enterprise has been supplying at least two different terrorist groups with arms over the past six years. The profits on those deals are tied up in that Van Gogh. If you sell it for them, liquidise their asset, you'll be in it up to your neck. We could put you away for the rest of your life.'

'Derek, I had no idea about all that. I was just trying to find out more on your behalf. A fishing expedition, isn't that what you guys call it? Look, maybe I pushed my luck, got a bit carried away. And if I screwed up, I apologise.'

'This is more than a screw-up, Al.'

'Oh, fuck. Is there something I can do to make things right?'

'Well, as it happens, there is. Something that if it works might just keep you out of jail. Here's what we need. You set the viewing up with Magna. Then you bring your guy and his adviser to view the picture. Except that the people who come with you won't actually be the representatives of this Middle Eastern collection.'

'Who will they be?'

'They'll be our guys.'

'What will they do then? If I lead them to the picture in the Freeport?'

'They'll take it from there.'

'Shit. That would finish me with the Magnas.'

'Believe me, Al, you don't want anything more to do with those gangsters. This is the least bad solution to your problems.'

## Thirteen

'So you didn't hit the jackpot after all?'

'Not this time.'

'Can't win them all, eh tiger?'

'So they say.'

'I've got news. I'm going abroad.'

'What, leaving London?'

'Yeah, going to be based in Mumbai. A year minimum. It's a great opportunity.'

'And what about us?'

'Look, it was fun while it lasted. We both knew it wasn't for ever.'

*The ending was embarrassingly weak, thought Melvyn, but he'd sort of got there. He could finesse the dialogue later. At least Alastair had got his come-uppance. The grasping bastard was well and truly scuppered. He might avoid jail, he might not. And best of all the girl friend was moving on. She was much, much too young for him – why couldn't he see that? The final scene could be worked on again tomorrow, but meanwhile Mona was coming round for dinner and had indicated that this time she might be disposed to stay the night. Melvyn felt a surge of such optimism that he put a bottle of champagne on ice. And tomorrow he would get cracking with the new chain saw. He needed to get out more, spend more of his day in the open air.*

*That machine was going to be his salvation. Goodbye unsightly oak branch. Hello bountiful quantities of fresh-cut and neatly stacked firewood. Not to mention page upon page of the novel he was about to start work on. The major work of literary fiction that would redefine his writing career.*

## Fourteen

*'Lethal, those powerful chain saws,' said the nurse in the Cottage Hospital the following day. She enjoyed treating accidents, particularly if there was a moral conclusion to be drawn from them. 'Lethal if you haven't got the experience, that is. Bloke just brought in here been trying to cut up a tree in his garden. Only gone and sliced off his index finger.'*

# Beautiful and Clever

'I'm really sorry, sir, I know I'm late for prayers, but I was reading a book and I lost all sense of time.'

'Lost all sense of time, Rollo, you young rogue? You don't honestly expect me to believe that, do you?' Mr Penwill cuffed the boy's head, but it was a cuffing that couldn't disguise its fondness, and the little thrill of excitement that the cuffer experienced as his hand came into contact with Rollo's floppy luxuriant hair.

Rollo sensed it. He knew these things, he knew them instinctively, even at twelve years old. He was in his last year at prep school. He was popular with his fellow pupils, he'd always been popular because he was good at games; but he was aware that the masters were interested in him too, prepared to cut him more slack than other boys, provided he smiled at them when he apologised for his latest misdemeanour. Because Rollo was not just good-looking, but eye-catchingly, heart-stoppingly good-looking. And he knew it. He knew where to draw the line, too. You didn't smile too engagingly at Mr Baines when Mr Baines loitered in the cricket pavilion instructing the older boys how to fit their protective boxes into their underpants before going out to bat. You kept a careful distance from Mr Baines.

'*Gyges, quem si puellarum insereres choro, mire sagaces falleret hospites.* Who'll translate? Rollo, what about you?' Mr Hargreaves was also on his case, pervy old Hargreaves the Latin master. But Rollo was very good at Latin, probably the best in the school.

'Gyges,' he said carefully, 'who if you put him in a chorus of girls, would deceive even the wise old men.'

'Good, good. In what way do you think Gyges deceived the wise old men?'

'I suppose because they thought he was a girl.' Rollo was determined not to give Hargreaves the satisfaction of seeing him blush.

'Why did they think that?'

'Because Gyges was a rather good-looking boy. Probably, sir.'

About the same time as he became aware of his own physical desirability, Rollo learned another good lesson. Which would he prefer, that the cricket first eleven, for whom he played as an opening batsman, should win with him making a duck, or lose comprehensively with him scoring 50? The latter, of course. There was no doubt in his mind. But the important lesson that he learned was that you should always pretend it was the other way about. Shake your head miserably as you walked off the pitch after defeat, when actually you were secretly exulting about your own half-century. Or exult ostentatiously at the team's victory, when inside you were furious at not scoring any runs yourself.

Rollo was lucky. Some boys who are beautiful at twelve or thirteen lose their looks by the time they're eighteen, as they thicken and coarsen. Gyges was probably one of them. But Rollo only got more beautiful on his journey through adolescence. Girls noticed. Boys noticed. Their mothers noticed, too. Helen Garland did, for sure.

Helen Garland was the mother of his friend Jacob. She was a divorcee and lived in a big house in Notting Hill. She drew her knuckles down the side of his face. Gently. But not too gently. I reckon I can loosen that muscle in your back for you, Rollo. Come round tomorrow and I'll get the massage table out. Jacob? Jacob will be away with his father for the next couple of days.

It seemed surprisingly natural, taking all his clothes off in front of her the next afternoon, even though he wasn't aware of any muscle in his back that needed loosening. Natural, too – or at least strangely inevitable – that she should also strip down to her underwear before their physical engagement. The only thing he hadn't been prepared for was how much noise she made. At first her panting and groaning was faintly embarrassing; and then suddenly her loss of control was the most exciting thing he'd ever experienced. As he walked home later, he felt two things: exultant, but conscious of the need to keep that exultance to himself. He'd scored 50, but his team had lost. It was two months before his sixteenth birthday.

Three years later he went up to Oxford where a coterie of queer dons in his college went weak-kneed at his company.

'May I get my gums round your plums?' suggested Dr Roger Foljambe, Bracegirdle Reader in Classical Philology, towards the end of a particularly vinous dessert in the Combination Room.

'I'd rather you didn't, actually, Roger,' replied Rollo.

'It's God's sense of humour, of course,' mused Dr Adrian Pretlove, Starkie Fellow in the History of Western Philosophy, refilling his port glass.

'What is?'

'To have arranged things so that the people you fancy never fancy you.'

Rollo said nothing. It wasn't a problem he had personally ever encountered. Still, he was not above an occasional mild flirtatiousness in his dealings with Foljambe, Pretlove and their circle; nothing physical, but a fluttering of his absurdly long eye-lashes, a toss of his glossy hair, and a mock-camp joke to send them all tittering away to their fevered fantasies behind their sported oaks. He knew how to get what he wanted out of people.

'And then of course God compounds the joke by inflict-ing on mankind an inbuilt preference for unfamiliar over fa-miliar flesh,' continued Pretlove, peeling a grape. 'Come to bed with me tonight, Rollo, and I'll be tired of you by tomorrow. I promise.'

This aspect of the divine sense of humour did strike a chord of recognition in Rollo. At Oxford he slept with a succession of beautiful girls but it was never long before seducing their best friends became more exciting than sticking with them.

'Would you rather be beautiful or clever?' one girl asked him in his last year. 'Yes, I know you're both, Rollo, but if you had to choose?'

'I'd rather be clever, of course,' he lied. He knew in his heart that if you were beautiful, you didn't have to be that clever to succeed. But if you were ugly you had to be very clever indeed. Being beautiful just made it all easier.

Gabriella de St Point was effortlessly, devastatingly beautiful. She was tall and perfectly proportioned with lustrous blond hair. Her mother was French and her father was Argentinian. She had been brought up in Paris, where by the time she was 23 she had been a successful model, acted in two films, and achieved an impressive law degree. Her good looks were transcendent: she used very little make-up and had the healthiest of appetites, being blessed with that capacity bestowed by Providence on only a few fortunate mortals (generally super-models) to eat and drink heartily without ever putting on weight. On top of that she was apparently immune to hangovers. Thus exempted from the physical anxieties and insecurities of the vast majority of womanhood, she turned inwards. Her interior life became of consuming importance to her.

*Il faut cultiver notre jardin*, she used to tell men she sat next to at dinner, and waited to see their reaction. Sometimes they caught the reference to Voltaire; more often it was the cue for them to drone on about garden architects and the size of their own estates in the country. She gave the impression not so much of boredom but of distance, as if she existed on a higher plane.

A higher plane of what? Of beauty of course, but that wasn't the point: in fact she defied people to judge her only by her beauty. It was an insult to her intelligence. No, she was in search of intensity, of spirituality, of sustenance for the soul. So she wrote poetry, played in a rock band called Blue Mist, and developed a small but genuine talent as a draughtsman. She drew the human figure with the tortured yet self-confident line of an Egon Schiele. One of her many admirers, a gallery owner in the Rue de Lille who eschewed socks, offered her an exhibition which she was wise enough to turn down.

She had been seventeen when she first went to bed with a man. He was in his forties, a friend of her mother's. He was killed in a car crash the next day, but he died happy. Gradually she began to disentangle from her subconscious the idea that sexual intercourse necessarily involved mortality. But it took some time, and she was cautious in her selection of subsequent lovers. They tended to be high-profile, as if their fame was some sort of insulation from reality: an Italian actor, a player in the French national football team; and then Maurice, an intellectual in his fifties who wore white open-necked shirts and was often on television, one of the ugliest men in France but one of the sexiest. A little to her surprise, all three survived the experience of intimacy with Gabriella without loss of life. But the actor turned out to be gay, the footballer took to drugs, and Maurice disappeared so far up himself as to be lost to her view.

Rollo met Gabriella in London when she was 27 and he was 28. They were both in the employ of separate American banks, each in negotiation with the other on behalf of their respective clients. As he watched her across the table of the meeting room in which he first encountered her he saw that her left profile was particularly lovely. Then she turned her head and he realised her right one was even better. She was already a vice-president, and evidently held in high regard by her colleagues, who tended to stop talking when she spoke and defer to her judgements. Rollo managed to exchange business cards with her. He had learned by experience the truth of Lord Chesterfield's maxim that, if you were dealing with either extreme female beauty or extreme female ugliness, it was best to flatter the lady concerned on the grounds of her intellect. So the next day he called Gabriella and told her he'd found her frighteningly intelligent and asked her out to dinner. She didn't really understand Englishmen: the examples she'd met so far were either emotionally constipated or boastfully self-satisfied. This one was good-looking, at least, but in the world in which Gabriella moved a good-looking man was about as unremarkable as a Catholic in the Vatican. Still, she accepted the invitation, on the basis that there might be some professional advantage to the contact. And what had Maurice once told her? People are like books, *ma chère*. None of them is so worthless that you can't learn something from them.

At dinner she said to Rollo, 'I think people are like books. None of them is so worthless that you can't learn something from them.'

'What are you going to learn from me?'

'That's up to you, *non*?'

Rollo laughed a worldly laugh. 'I don't think I can probably teach you very much. You're too clever for me.'

She smiled and said nothing. She correctly interpreted his self-deprecation as false modesty. He incorrectly interpreted her reticence as veiled desire.

'We could have a drink in my flat,' he suggested as they left the restaurant.

She shook her head. 'I have a breakfast with a client at eight tomorrow morning. Thank you for the delicious dinner.'

It was such an unfamiliar response that for a moment he thought he had misheard her. Or that she was teasing him. He had never for one moment doubted that the evening would end up with her accompanying him home to his flat, and once there into his bed. It was how countless other nights had unfolded. It was how things worked. But she swiftly hailed a taxi, kissed him on both cheeks and then he was alone there, just standing on the pavement.

He decided to walk home. He needed time to think. He reflected that there were some games when you not only failed to score a run yourself, but your team were also comprehensively defeated. It was a salutary revelation. He was approaching the block of flats where he lived when he heard the voice of a passer-by calling his name from the other side of the street.

'Rollo? I thought it was you.'

She was a middle-aged blond woman, bulky, wearing rather too much lipstick. She looked faintly familiar. 'Don't tell me you've forgotten me. Helen Garland.'

She wasn't entirely sober. Nor was he. Her availability impinged on him like a sudden escape of gas. He did hesitate, just for a moment. But then he reflected that, if you'd just failed as a batsman in a big game, it made good sense at the earliest opportunity to knock up a big score against inferior bowling. He heard his own voice saying, 'Hey, great to see you again. Fancy a drink? I live just in here, actually.' In the lift up to his flat she ran her knuckles down his cheek.

Afterwards, as she was putting her clothes back on, she said, 'Your trouble, Rollo, is that you're just too beautiful for your own good.'

She stood looking in the mirror as she reapplied lipstick. They were both sober now. 'Thank you for fitting me in,' she said. 'I suppose you have lots of girlfriends.'

'No,' he said. 'Just one. She's called Gabriella and she's away in Paris on business tonight. I'm very much in love with her.'

'My good luck, then.'

'What?'

'To catch you when she's out of town.'

He went downstairs with her and hailed her a taxi. As it drew up he asked, 'How's Jacob?'

'He's doing very well. He's a fully qualified doctor now.'

'Wow. Well done him.' He opened the taxi door for her. 'So, see you around.'

'So long, Rollo. Give my love to Gabriella.'

When Gabriella got home the same evening Verna was already in bed. Verna was a Danish super-model, even taller than Gabriella and almost as beautiful. Gabriella slid in next to her.

'*Ça va?*' Verna murmured, '*Tu as passé une soirée merveilleuse?*'

'*Assez ennuyeuse,*' said Gabriella. She kissed Verna's ear and they went to sleep with their long legs entwined.

# Champions

The pain came in sharp, jagged waves, insolent in its intensity. Coping with it demanded his entire physical and mental focus. There was barely energy left in him to press the button that summoned the nurse. But later, when the morphine had taken its effect and he was lying in bed calmer, a kind of fog drifted in and out of his brain which made it difficult to distinguish between what was real and what was dream. One evening there seemed to be a party going on at the nurses' station just along the corridor from his room. There was definitely the clink of glasses, possibly the pop of a champagne cork, and the sound of voices making arrangements for dinner later. Would Steve join them? Where was Steve? Who was Steve? Once he saw a batsman walking through his room; a batsman going out to bat, fully padded up and wearing a helmet. Another time he was sure there was a dog under his bed, snuffling around and causing a commotion with its tail just like Hector used to. Then the fog drifted in again.

He couldn't read for more than a few minutes at a time, he couldn't take it in, he couldn't focus on the sequences of words. Sentences suddenly changed, didn't hold together, finished off quite different from how they'd started. And the television, fixed high on the wall opposite his bed, only confused him when it was on. The images came too quickly, he couldn't follow them, the effort of watching was too great, so he'd asked them to leave it disconnected. Its screen now loomed down over him, faintly menacing in its blindness. Then there was his mobile telephone. He'd never liked the thing, never properly understood it. The noises it made had always alarmed him, even after Gus had taught him how to send messages on it, how to go onto the internet to get information. But it was all too much for him now. It lay there, next to his bed, resolutely switched off. The only things he still occasionally managed to pull over his head were his earphones. He listened to audiobooks, and sometimes he listened to music, too. But the audiobooks and the music mostly sent him off to sleep. Oh no. Here comes the pain again. Jagged, surging. Just concentrate. Concentrate. Reach out to call the nurse. Morphine. Blessed morphine.

Gus. Sometimes Gus was there. He liked Gus being there. Gus was the only one he could talk to about Chelsea. It was the one thing that galvanised him, the Chelsea score, what they'd done this week, who they were playing next. It had always been like that, as if he was hard-wired to his team. His support for them was at the centre of his being, defining him. It was atavistic, a bit like a religion. His own father had first taken him to watch Chelsea back in the early fifties, and he had followed them ever since. Then he had started taking Gus in the nineties, when the boy was eight, and Gus had quickly developed into an equally ardent fan. But they let you down, Chelsea, they always did. Like this week. It had all been going so well, they'd just beaten Manchester United, they'd moved up to third in the table; and then they'd lost at home to Villa. It hurt. Not like the jagged, surging pain that engulfed him in this hospital. But the wound of defeat was a low, dispiriting, lingering thing and it cast him down. It cast him down disproportionately. It always had, but somehow even more now in this place where he had time to brood on it. Ginny had told him he was ridiculous to mind so much. And now you're infecting your own son, she'd said. Look at Gus, he minds as much as you do. You and your bloody Chelsea. Darling Ginny. She had understood everything about him. But not that. Or wait a minute: perhaps she'd even understood that too.

It was Gus speaking to him. Look, Dad, he was saying. I've set up a special mobile for you. So you can get the Chelsea score. Just click it on and off. It's a football site, gives you updates. He said he didn't want the complication, he didn't understand all that technical stuff. It's not complicated, Dad. Look, Dan and I set it up for you. Actually Dan did most of it. Ten years old and he's a technological genius, knows more than I do and I'm meant to be the expert. You just press this to put it on. Then there you are, the latest football news on the screen. I don't want all that news, I can't take it in. But you want the football scores, you want to know what Chelsea have done, don't you? A long pause. The fog was thickening, but it suddenly cleared for a moment.

Yes, he agreed, he wanted to know what Chelsea had done, of course he did. But none of the other stuff. Just football. No politics and wars and bombs and stock markets, he didn't want that. Just football. You've got it, Dad. Just football, just the premier league. That's all it will give you, nothing else. Results and news updated each day. Just press this button, on and off. Everything you need to know will come up on the screen. He sighed. He felt very tired. But he felt a warmth suffusing him, at what Gus and Dan had done for him. Gus his son; Dan his grandson. Working together to set it up for him. It made him slightly tearful to think of it. They were good boys. They were clever boys. Dan was so like Gus, sometimes he called Dan Gus; they had become interchangeable, Dan and the Gus of thirty years ago.

Thanks, Gus, he had murmured. I think I need a little sleep now. OK Dad, you get some rest. But remember, just a touch of the button when you want Chelsea news. The latest results, the fixtures and the table. Nothing more than that, couldn't be simpler. At your fingertips. As Gus made his way out, he had dragged a hand from beneath the sheet and waved it in a gesture of silent gratitude and farewell. And then he heard his own voice asking, who is it this weekend? Gus paused in the doorway and said calmly, Leeds. Leeds away. Tough one, he murmured back. And then the fog closed in again.

Through the rest of the week the upcoming match at Leeds played on his mind even more than usual. Because he knew he would have immediate access to the final score, and because Gus and Dan had set that access up for him, the process of revelation that would take place in the late afternoon of Saturday assumed a heightened significance. He watched the days and hours pass on the little digital clock on his bedside table. Thursday and Friday came and went, and then with the familiar little shudder of anticipation that he always felt on mornings in the football season when Chelsea were playing, he awoke to Saturday. He lay there with the fog coming and going, focusing on only one thing: when he pressed the button on his new mobile around 17.00, he would get the final score. It would just come up on the screen, Gus had assured him. Anticipation and anxiety rose and fell in him through the fog of the morning. And then around lunchtime the jagged remorseless pain surged up through his body again. They gave him morphine. When he awoke later the first thing he did was look at the clock. 16.43. Gingerly, he measured the distance he would have to move his hand to reach the mobile. The pain was much less now. Yes, he could do it. But not yet. They would still be playing, into the final ten minutes. As he knew from past experience, it was better not to check till it was all over, when there was nothing you could do about it. But now the anxiety about the score was suddenly acute. Don't let them lose. On top of all else, he couldn't take the pain of Chelsea losing. Not now, when he felt so weak. Not now, when he found tears welling up in his eyes at the thought of defeat. A grown man crying at a football result, it was pathetic. Still, maybe a draw? 1-1 wouldn't be a bad result, away from home. Yes, he'd take 1-1. He'd be happy at 1-1.

At 16.59 he reached out for the machine and as he did so, he thought of Gus and Dan, also reaching out, getting the final score on their mobiles. They were all joined, hard-wired together. All three of them.

He touched the button, just like Gus had told him, and then there it was, jumping off the screen at him: Leeds 0, Chelsea 3. That was an incredible result. It was as if a new drip had been fixed to his arm and its tendril was pumping him through with surges of pure elation. He managed to scroll down the screen a little further to check the table. Chelsea had gone up from 3rd to 2nd. He switched off. He had read enough. He lay back on the pillow. He felt very, very tired. But very, very tired in a good way.

That was quite a score, he said to Gus when he came in the next day. 3-0. Away from home. Yes, Gus said, not bad was it. Now we're only three points off top place. It was late April already: as he lay in bed he could see leaves budding on the trees through his window. How many more games? We've played 35. Three more. Are we going to do it? Could we do it? Win the league again? He remembered Gus's teenage excitement the first time it had happened, the intensity of his pleasure, the way the boy had looked at him with a wordless gratitude, as if his father had done it for him personally, as if he had given Gus the greatest present in the world.

Look, 83 isn't old, dad, Gus was telling him.

Your mother died when she was 74. I'm past my sell-by date.

Don't talk nonsense. There's plenty still to live for.

They both knew what that plenty was: nothing less than the premier league championship. The championship, one more time.

The fog was coming in again, but there was something he must remind Gus. Something he'd said so many times before but needed to be said again now. To protect him; to protect both of them. Gus, he said, remember: it's not the despair that gets you down. It's the hope.

It was Everton at home that Wednesday. The games were coming thick and fast as they always did at this end of the season. He had morphine for the pain early in the evening when they were playing, so it wasn't till 3 a.m. on Thursday morning that he woke up sufficiently to reach for the mobile. At night the whole hospital was bathed in this strange submarine greenness. You lay there and heard the distant throb of monitors, interspersed with the occasional bleep of alarms. They were impersonal noises, as if there were no human beings left, only machines. There was never a moment when the place was totally quiet. He pressed the button and the score swam into his consciousness with a little flourish of relief and delight: Chelsea 2 Everton 1. And Arsenal had only drawn at Tottenham. That meant Chelsea were just one point off the top. One point, with two to play. The numbers swirled in his brain, so he couldn't fix them anymore. But as he lapsed back into sleep, it was a sleep of imprecise contentment.

In the days following he went through a bad patch. He descended into a measureless sequence of dreams and nightmares and surges of pain. Once Ginny came to the window and was knocking on the glass. But though he shouted to her, she didn't hear him. He lost all understanding of where he was, or what he was doing; there was a vague anxiety about a flight he had to catch, about meetings in the office he had missed. And then, at some indeterminate time later, there was Gus. Gus, thank God, standing by his bed. The fog cleared. You had us a bit worried there, Dad, Gus was saying. He smiled in Gus's direction. I'm OK, he said, because he knew that was what Gus wanted to hear. The fog drifted clear for a moment. What day is it? He asked. Sunday. Sunday afternoon. Aren't we? I mean, Chelsea? Yes, six o'clock kick-off, Gus said. Newcastle away. Check on your mobile later, Dad.

When he woke up again it was nine in the evening. It was a natural instinct now to reach for his mobile, the one thing he was good at, the one thing he remembered how to do. Newcastle 0 Chelsea 1, it told him. And Arsenal had only drawn again. There they were, Chelsea, on top of the table. By one point. It came to him the next morning, in a moment of unexpected and unaccustomed clarity: win our last game and we've won the league. It doesn't matter what Arsenal or anyone else does. As long as we beat West Ham, we're there. Champions. By this time next week we'll know. By this time next week it will all be over.

The hospital rang Gus at 4.30 on the Monday morning seven days later. Come at once, they said. He's not got long. He's sunk into a coma. Gus was with him when he died, was actually holding his hand when he felt him go. It was 7.46 a.m.: Gus happened to note the time on his father's digital clock on his bedside table. The mobile was lying there too, and a little later Gus picked it up. He went to the window. Early May. The chestnut trees outside were approaching full bloom. He clicked the mobile on. It went straight through to the site that he and Dan had set up. There it was, the score that surely his father must have seen, that would have made him die happy. Chelsea 2, West Ham 0. Followed by the final table, with Chelsea proudly at the top, crowned champions.

He asked the nurse how his father had been the previous evening. When had he lost consciousness? She couldn't say exactly, but she had come in as usual at 6.30 to take his pulse and check his morphine levels and he'd been awake then. How had he been at 6.30? He was smiling, he was good.

Smiling. Of course he had been smiling. Because he had hung on just long enough to reach out and click the button on his mobile. To reach out and see the score against West Ham. Gus slipped the mobile into his coat pocket. It had fulfilled its function, communicating the alternative reality that he and Dan had constructed so laboriously, the fabricated Chelsea results that they had been feeding through to his father's screen over the past three weeks.

Loved his football, didn't he, your Dad? The nurse was continuing as she folded blankets. My Geoff, he's an Arsenal fan. A Gunner through and through. I remember now, I told your Dad my Geoff would be celebrating tonight.

What? You told him Arsenal had won the League?

I did. Thought he'd like to know.

And… and how did he react?

He didn't say anything. He just smiled. He was a sweet man, your Dad.

# The Family Restorer

The first time I saw the portrait it made me uneasy. The composition was awkward, but there was more to it than that. The sitters seemed unsympathetic: a man and a woman, presumably husband and wife, in a shadowy interior. Their costume was late eighteenth century, and the room in which they stood reasonably grand. I didn't like them. I didn't like the pinched, furtive, almost fearful look in her eyes. And as for him, he stared aggressively out at you, defying any suggestion that all was not well with him, with his wife, with his household, with his horses, with his parkland just visible through the window beyond.

'A new acquisition?' I pulled away the blanket in which the picture had been loosely wrapped, and glanced up at the owner. Sir Marcus stood there straight-backed amid the chaos of my studio, in amongst the brushes, the bottles, the powerful magnifying lamps, the pervasive smell of white spirit and turpentine. He wore an ancient tweed suit and looked exactly what he was, the countryman dressed for a rare London visit; out of breath after carrying the painting up in the lift, and slightly disorientated. He was a widower, I remembered, and no longer a young man.

'That's right.' He spoke gruffly. 'I bought it at auction six months or so ago.'

'Ah. I thought I hadn't seen it at Howland.' I had visited his lovely Cotswold manor house two or three times, to advise on the picture collection. There were some unusually good things there, as a matter of fact, and I had done quite a bit of conservation work for him. Originally I'd been a friend of his daughter Mary. Now I was the family's tame restorer.

'Rather pleased with it, actually,' he went on. 'Bit of a find. It's Sir Thomas, the fifth baronet, and his wife. There's an old inscription on the reverse. As far as we can make out that's the drawing room at Howland, too. I think we've still got that mirror. And the panelling's recognisable.'

'So it is. How fascinating.'

'I've lived with it for a month or two, hung it in the gallery outside the bedroom. Now I've decided I'd like to have it cleaned.'

'You're right, there's a lot of dirt and old varnish on it. It should come up well. With a bit of luck we'll be able to see a good deal more of the drawing room once that's off.'

He nodded, and there was a pause. I wondered if I should offer him a drink. After all he was a good client. I had some gin somewhere, but I also kept the white spirit in a gin bottle and didn't want to run the risk of a confusion. He gave a little cough and added: 'Thought I'd drop it in myself as I had to come up to town anyway. Got an appointment in Harley Street in half an hour.'

'Nothing serious, I hope?'

He laughed mirthlessly. ''Old age, I suppose. Can't seem to sleep. Mary said I should come and have myself looked at. Keep hearing things, you see, hearing things in my head. Started just recently. All sorts of odd noises, often sounds like children crying. But it can't be, aren't any children in the house. Not now, not any more…' His voice trailed away, and for a moment he looked puzzled, as if he had glimpsed something inexpressible, incomprehensible. Then abruptly he pulled himself together. 'Nothing to it, of course,' he said firmly. 'I'm perfectly fit.' You could hear his back straightening up again. He stared at me, challenging me to deny his good health. Across the centuries that look of assertive aggression was momentarily familiar. I thought suddenly, is he dying, I wonder?

I live above the shop. That's to say my studio is incorporated into my flat. It's good security, apart from anything else. The insurers like to know I'm never far away when there are valuable pictures locked up there overnight. My bedroom's just across the passage from the studio door. And I'm high up there on the fifth floor, with spectacular views of the rooftops of London.

I went to bed about eleven that night. It had been a long day and I was tired. Normally I'm an excellent sleeper, but I awoke suddenly at about quarter to three in the morning.

I was unaccountably terrified. I lay there, sick and cold with fear. For a moment I couldn't grasp whether what was frightening me was dreamed or real. Then I heard it again: a sharp, plangent, horrifying cry. It went right through you, cut you to the very quick, like the cry of a young child in pain. No. That was ridiculous. It must be some wretched cat out on the roof. An acoustical trick made it sound very close, almost as if it was coming from the studio. I was conscious of my heart beating, suddenly reminded of the sensation of a childhood nightmare.

Then the wailing came again, disconcertingly close, infinitely sad. Was it a cat? The third time I knew it wasn't. It was a child crying. I drew myself out of bed and padded slowly across to the studio door. I unlocked it and peered in. Everything was silent. The Flemish landscape I was working on still stood there on the easel. Bottles and brushes littered the tables and shelves undisturbed. Against the wall where I had left it leaning I could make out Sir Marcus's portrait of his forebears.

On each of the two following nights I heard the crying again but could not trace it. I listened miserably to the heart-rending sound. And the more I heard it the more it seemed to me to be a cry compounded not just of pain but of fear and frustration. The cry of a child locked in the dark somewhere, a child who cannot get out.

By the fourth day it was getting to me. I was tired, irritable, and unnerved. I was beginning to wonder if I shouldn't seek some sort of help. I decided to try to break the routine, and instead of working went for a long walk in Hyde Park. At lunchtime I came back to the studio, laid aside the Flemish landscape and made a start on Sir Marcus's picture.

It was very dirty indeed. I began at the upper left corner and working towards the centre succeeded in revealing a lot more detail of the room. It was a satisfying painting to clean, being in rather better state than I had suspected, and I surrendered to the absorption of the process. But moving down to the bottom right quadrant I was surprised to find a large area of overpaint. Normally overpaint covers up damage. Tentatively I removed a little, then a little more. Strange. It was obscuring perfectly good original paint as far as I could see. Gradually it all came away. And then there it was. Or there he was, I should say. A little boy, playing on the floor at his parents' feet. A little boy of two or three years old. The age when they cry a lot at night. The age when they first start being frightened by the dark.

I finished cleaning off the overpaint. I worked with an urgency, eager to release the child from his shroud of blackness, to give him back to the light. Now the picture itself made more sense. Perhaps the man's aggressiveness was no more than paternal pride; and the woman's look not so much furtive as anxious, suggesting maternal concern.

Anyway, there was no crying that night. I slept a blissful, uninterrupted sleep and awoke much refreshed.

Sir Marcus himself came to pick the picture up a couple of weeks later.

'What an extraordinary thing,' he said as he peered perplexed at the child on the floor. 'There's no record of any offspring. They were always understood to have died childless. Howland and the title passed to the nephew, Sir Frederick, the sixth baronet.'

'Perhaps there was a son who died young,' I suggested.

He shrugged, then smiled at me. 'Anyway, it's come up damned well. You've done a good job.' He seemed relaxed, much less tense than on his last visit.

'Everything was OK with the doctor?' I asked.

'Tintinitis, or some such bloody silly name. That's what I think he said it was. Anyway the trouble's gone now, went just like that, the moment I consulted him. Got home and slept soundly ever since. Always the way, isn't it?'

I nodded. I was half inclined to add a charge for medical services to my own restoration bill.

I heard no more of Sir Marcus until nearly a year later when I read of his death in the paper. On the spur of the moment I drove down to the funeral.

After the service we trooped back to Howland. I had forgotten quite how beautiful the house was. I wandered into the drawing room, and was idly running my eye over the panelling and a suddenly familiar mirror when Mary pressed a cup of tea into my hand.

'It was a release really,' she said. 'Poor old boy, he kept hearing things. It was driving him mad.'

'Hearing things? What sort of things?'

'That was the odd part of it, he would never really tell me. Not until last week, that is, the day before he died. He said what he heard was a child's voice, every night, giving him no rest.'

'Oh my God. What, crying you mean?'

She looked at me, surprised. 'No, singing and laughing he said. Constantly singing and laughing.'

# Hannay Meets
Chatterley

I had always promised myself, once the show with Germany was over and my soldiering days were done, that I would fetch up in the English countryside. It was something of a dream of mine, a vision that kept me going under the relentless African sun, in many a tight spot in the Balkans, and through the dark days and nights of the trenches at Mons. Now here I was, Major Richard Hannay, master of my own greystone manor house and steward of a goodly spread of green acres. In so far as providence allows to human beings a measure of contentment, I felt I had received more than my fair share. It was a still bright afternoon, with a slight haze to temper the glare of the sun. Sandy and I set off on a cross-country tramp, dipping into the valley below to follow the course of the river. The banks were delicious, full of the scents of mints and meadow-sweet, yellow flag-irises glowing by the water's edge, and the first dog-roses beginning to star the hedges. Then we struck into woodland along a path as ancient as England herself. It was good to be alive, relishing the open air, and savouring the companionship that only another man can give, another man tested and tempered by the same kind of challenges as life has thrown your own way too.

Let me tell you about Sandy Arbuthnott. If you consult the Peerage you will find that to Edward Cospatrick, fifteenth Baron Clanroyden, there was born in the year 1882, as his second son, Ludovic Gustavus Arbuthnott, commonly called the Honourable, etc., educated at Eton and New College, Oxford. What it doesn't say is that he's tallish, with a lean high-boned face and a pair of brown eyes like a pretty girl's. He's not the chap to buck about himself, but I'd rather have him in my corner than any other fellow on God's earth. He's knocked about the world from Mecca to Samarkand, from Cairo to the Veldt; his skin may be bronzed by countless southern suns, but he's the whitest man alive.

As we walked, we exchanged yarns and reminisced about odd places and people we had in common. We have been in a fair few scrapes, Sandy and I, and weathered them as much by luck as by judgement. We think alike. We value the same things. Neither of us has ever been tempted to throw his weight behind the Suffragette movement, for instance. By the same token, we have little truck with the posturings of poets and our spirits instinctively recoil from those neurasthenic types of the manmillinery persuasion. Nor will you find us at the front of the queue to purchase tickets for the *Ballet Russe*. But give either of us God's wide-open acres, throw in a gun and a quarry worthy of our mettle, be it furred or feathered, and we are happy as sandboys.

In a clearing we came upon a game-keeper's hut. Some sudden premonition of evil alighted, I think, on both of us at that moment, like a bird of ill omen. The sun dappled through the branches as we instinctively crouched, alert, in the undergrowth. I edged forward. The door was shut, and a strange noise emanated from within. In my days as a mining engineer I spent many hard but rewarding hours beneath an African sun dredging diamonds, gold and iron ore from the unforgiving depths of the earth. What I heard reminded me of those times: the repetitious thud of a piece of piston-driven machinery, rising and falling in spasms of relentless energy. I peered in through a window, then turned away in shock.

'Sandy, keep back.'

'What is it?'

'Run and fetch a bucket of clean honest water from yonder stream.'

'Why, Dick?

'There's a man and a woman committing an act of beastliness in this hut. If we tip cold water over them we can put a stop to their filth.'

'Very well, Dick.'

'Good God, it's Lady Chatterley, Sir Clifford's wife.'

'Still need the bucket?'

'Cancel the bucket, Sandy. Ah, good afternoon, Constance. Lovely weather for April. No, no, don't get up. What a charming flower arrangement. Mellors, don't just sit there, put something over her Ladyship. And over yourself too, man.'

The gamekeeper eyed me oddly, even a trifle resentfully. 'Thou wert previous,' he said.

'Previous?'

'Has a will of his own, does John Thomas. Once he be set going, there be no good standing in his way.'

'Now look here, Mellors, I don't know who this sportsman John Thomas is, but I don't want to hear any more of your impertinence. Very best to Sir Clifford, Constance. We must be getting along.'

Sandy and I continued our walk. Neither of us spoke for many minutes.

I was reflecting on the fair sex. The truth is that women have never much crossed my path, and I know about as much of their ways as I know about the Chinese language. My life has been lived largely with men, and rather a rough crowd at that. The soft cushions and the subtle scents of womanhood fill me with acute uneasiness. I remember an evening in Paris before the war which I was compelled to spend, in the service of my country, in the sort of dubious establishment of which our Gallic cousins seem to make rather a speciality, where the lights are as low as the morals. I was offered a poisonous brew called absinthe, but I insisted on good honest Scotch whisky instead. Presently a girl came on the stage and danced, a silly affair, all a clashing of tambourines and wriggling. I have seen native women do the same thing better in a Mozambique kraal. I ordered more whisky to steady my hand. Then I noticed that a lady had joined me at my table. Although we hadn't been introduced, good manners demanded that I offer her refreshment. She requested champagne. Once the bottle stood there in its ice bucket, it seemed churlish not to join her in a glass or two.

Half an hour later I felt I had waited long enough. The dago blackguard I was meant to be shadowing did not look as though he was going to put in an appearance that night. I called for *l'addition*, paid it, and left the premises. I flagged down a motor cab and was just settling myself in the back seat when I found that the lady of my recent acquaintance had somehow entered the cab with me and was arranging herself at my side. I don't think that I had ever been in a motor car with a lady before. At first I felt like a fish on a dry sandbank. But then a number of things conspired to exert a strange and demonic effect; perhaps it was the confined space, the softness of the upholstery, or even the action of the champagne coming on top of the whisky, but all at once passion was beating in the air – terrible savage passion, which belonged neither to day nor night, life nor death, but to the half-world between them. I suddenly felt as if a stick of dynamite had been planted at the very centre of me, primed and ready to explode. Worse, the she-devil's gloved hand had edged its way on to my thigh, in very narrow proximity to the danger area. Another inch or two and I couldn't have answered for the consequences. I summoned all my willpower and leant forward to tap on the partition. Just in time I told the driver to pull over at once. 'Madam,' I said to her as I left the vehicle, 'I think you have mistaken me for someone else. I am a British officer.'

It was Sandy who finally broke the silence. We had emerged from the woodland and were back on the riverbank, retracing our steps. 'Dick,' he said, 'did you ever hear of a thing called the Superman?'

'There was a time when the papers were full of nothing else,' I answered. 'I gather it was invented by a sportsman called Nietzsche.'

'There never has been and there never could be a real Superman.'

'You don't think so?'

'Emphatically not. But there might be a Superwoman. Women have got a perilous logic which we never have, and some of the best of them don't see the joke of life like the ordinary man. But they can be more entirely damnable than anything that was ever breeched, for they don't stop still now and then and laugh at themselves. When the Superwoman comes, we must all run for cover.'

'It does me good to hear your voice, Sandy,' I said. 'It reminds me of clean, honest things.'

We walked on. Sometimes silence between men is more eloquent than any amount of chatter with women. Only as we reached the familiar gates of home and made our way up the drive did Sandy speak again.

'I knew you were upset back there. Because of something you said.'

'What?'

'You said yonder. Yonder stream.'

'I would never say yonder.'

'But you did.'

'By all that's holy, what do you take me for? One of those limp-wristed wretches who come over all archaic at the joys of the English countryside?'

'Absolutely not, Dick. That's why when you said yonder it showed how upset you were. Not yourself.'

I paused. And it was at that moment that a quite appalling thought came to mind.

'I've just remembered something, Sandy.'

'What?'

'Clifford and Connie are coming to dinner tonight.'

'The Chatterleys? Good God.'

'It seemed a neighbourly thing to do to invite them. Knowing you were staying.'

'Well, of course they'll cry off now. She couldn't possibly… I mean, not after…'

At that point we reached the front door where Venables was waiting for us. 'I have just had Lady Chatterley on the tele-phone line, sir,' he said. 'She wanted to know what time she and Sir Clifford are expected. I took the liberty of telling her 7.30 for 8 as usual.'


'Connie tells me she bumped into you two this afternoon.'

I turned the colour of the claret. 'Yes indeed, Clifford. Only briefly. We were out on a ramble.'

'And she was doing this and that with Mellors. Damned good man, Mellors.'

'Excellent gamekeeper, I'm sure,' I said in a faint voice.

'He's good at other things, too,' said his wife. She looked straight at me, unwavering.

I made a motion with my hands to indicate that I would not argue with her assessment.

'He knows about flowers as well as birds.'

I had a sudden vision of the garland of meadowsweet; the garland somewhat the worse for wear, but still visible woven into the birds nest at her groin that afternoon. 'How are the pheasants doing this year?' I asked Sir Clifford.

'Splendid,' he said.

Very little port was drunk that evening. It was barely ten o'clock when Sir Clifford turned awkwardly in his wheelchair, grimaced and confessed that the old war wound was giving him gyp. 'No good to man or beast in this state,' he apologized as Connie wheeled him out into the drive where his chauffeur was waiting with the car. 'Damned sporting of you to have us, though.'

As he went up to bed that night, Sandy paused on the stairs. 'Rum do,' he murmured. That was all he said.

# Duplicity

Despite the air conditioning, the man sitting one down from me at the bar of Raffles Hotel was regularly wiping the sweat from his forehead with a large silk handkerchief. He was overweight and didn't look well. But he retained the vestige of something distinguished: his shirt was expensive, and he wore a gold signet ring on his little finger. I am a connoisseur of degrees of inebriation and I reckoned this guy was just emerging from the introverted stage. He'd had the first three or four drinks alone and was now primed for conversation; the final stage would be self-revelation, and possibly tears, which you didn't necessarily hang around for. I'd seen plenty like him before. I was no stranger to hotel bars myself and knew that this was the dangerous hour, just past midnight, when the truly monumental bores come out of hiding to parade their paranoias and their conspiracy theories and the maudlin depths of their self-pity. You engaged with them at your peril.

He turned to face me and briefly flashed a smile of unexpected charm. 'You're looking at a man on the edge,' he said.

'I'm sorry to hear that.'

'Everyone's past catches up with them in the end. Your sins will find you out.'

'So they say.'

'The important thing is to be practical now. Think logically. I may be a moral coward, but I hope I'm not a physical one.' He stared thoughtfully into his whisky glass, as if he wasn't quite sure whether he'd said it right. 'Anyway, I'm looking into extradition treaties, I mean countries that don't have them with the US.'

'Brazil?' I hazarded.

'Uh uh. No good anymore. There's an agreement in place with Brazil now. But there's still Morocco, Indonesia, the Maldives.' He counted them off on his fingers.

'Could be worse. Is the trouble you're in really that bad?'

'You want to hear about it?'

He was signalling to the barman to refill both our whisky glasses, so the least I could do was listen. Besides, I sensed something different about him, something beyond the bravado of the alcohol, an underlying coherence that commanded attention and yes, a degree of credibility. Some of it might be exaggeration and self-aggrandisement, but I was intrigued. And I'd had quite a lot to drink myself, too, by that time.

'I'm an art dealer, you see,' he began. 'Not an unsuccessful one in my time. About five years ago I was here in Singapore, and I came across this little guy called Ho. He had a studio out in the country, if you can call anywhere the country in this urban jungle. Anyway, he was a technological genius. You know this three-dimensional printing that replicates things? Well, he'd taken it further than I'd imagined possible, and he'd done it with paintings. Put it like this, I'd defy the best expert in the world to tell the difference between the original and the copy that this guy generated. Of course the original had to be modern: what he couldn't manage was to replicate age. I mean Rembrandt wasn't on the menu. But late Picasso, late Chagall, things done in the last fifty or sixty years, they were prime candidates.

'I was smart. I act quickly when I see an opportunity, always have. I drew up an agreement with Mr Ho, that he would work for me exclusively from then on. I paid him a hefty enough retainer. And the thing about Mr Ho was he loved the technology. He really loved what he was doing in that studio of his. He wasn't really interested in the money, except as a means of continuing his life's work.

'I had a project in mind. As scams went it was a good one, as long as you didn't look too far ahead. OK, the further into the future I projected likely outcomes the more perilous the enterprise became. But in the short to medium term it was simple and it was effective. After the initial investment there would be substantial returns, almost immediately. I calculated that with any kind of luck I'd got a good five to ten years of substantial regular earning ahead of me. And after that? Well, who wants to see further than that anyway?

'So this is what I did. I raised the cash to buy a small late Picasso. I bought it in New York at public auction in that November five or six years ago. It's totally kosher. You know, one of those slapdash ones, brush loaded with paint splurged across the canvas, leaving downward dribbles at arbitrary intervals. And on the reverse there was the date, I'll never forget it: 25.10.71, in the artist's unmistakable handwriting. This was the sort of painting that Picasso didn't need more than a day to do, more likely just an hour, or maybe even less than that, maybe a matter of minutes. Have a look, here's an image on Artnet.' He brought out his I-phone and, with a surprisingly assured touch for a man who'd had as much to drink as he had, summoned up the relevant page from the many millions of works of art recorded on the website of prices. 'Look, there it is: Lot 47 on 13 November at Christie's that year. I paid $3.5 million for it. That's my Picasso, dated 25.10.71. No mistaking it. Recorded for ever in that bible of ultimate truth, the internet.

'Three months later I sold it to this guy in Shanghai, by name of Benny Chen. He was a client I'd dealt with before, stinking rich, knew nothing about art but just wanted to diversify his investments and liked the name Picasso. I sold it to him for $3.8 million. He was happy to give me that small mark up because he could look on Artnet and be reassured that the authenticity and the price of the picture he was buying was validated by its recent sale at international auction. And I'd got my money back, with a modest commission on top. So everyone's happy, no?

'But before I despatched it to Benny Chen, I gave it to Ho to work his magic on. And within a couple of days he'd produced a duplicate. I tell you what came out took my breath away – it was a totally identical picture: it wasn't the sort of painting that even the most skillful human copyist could reproduce with total accuracy. Spontaneity like that was not humanly replicable, not so that you got the drips of paint to fall and congeal in exactly the same places. But Ho had done it, with his technology. I put the two works side by side and they were identical, absolutely nothing between them, down to the sweep of the brushstroke and the dripping of the paint and the inscription of the date on the reverse. I don't mind telling you that I couldn't tell them apart. Fucking marvellous. You know something? I'm still not sure which one I sent off to Benny Chen, the original or the replica. But I figured it actually didn't matter.

'The remaining version I kept for eighteen months, then I consigned it back to Christie's New York for their summer sale. As far as Christie's were concerned it was the picture I'd bought from them the previous October. They put it up for auction and then I trousered again.' He reached for his I-phone and scrolled down a few pages. 'Look, here it is on Artnet again, sold on 10 May the year after. The same picture. Ah, the joy of the rising market for Picasso! I got $4 million this time. $4 million of pure profit. That was very substantial gravy.'

I said, 'Weren't you worried that your guy in Shanghai might notice his picture coming up for sale again in Christie's, when as far as he was concerned it was hanging on his wall?'

'No. Benny Chen didn't look at his pictures. He just stuck them away in a high-security warehouse and forgot about them. He was in it for the long term. He didn't follow the sales at the international auction houses, certainly not in detail. His game-plan was to hang on to a painting like the Picasso for at least ten years. That's the way you get the best return in the modern art market, after all. I'd dinned that into him.

'So I thought about it. Do I push my luck again? Or maybe just run for the hills? But I still had Ho in my exclusive employment. It seemed a waste not to make use of him while I could. So I took the money I'd got for the Picasso to start the process again. This time it was a Chagall that I bought, at Sotheby's for $2.8 million. I got it identically copied by Ho, then I sold it twice again, once privately to Benny Chen and once a year later trading it in at international auction at Sotheby's as before. It was a great formula. I did it twice more, with another Picasso and a Fontana. I was lucky, you see. Benny Chen was making zillions out of his gaming empire and was keen to expand his art holdings. The market was rising, and he kept buying from me and stashing the stuff away.'

The barman asked us if we wanted more whisky. We did. My companion put the glass to his lips and sighed. 'All good things come to an end, I guess,' he went on, 'but somehow I'd lulled myself into the belief that I was untouchable. And then out of the blue I got these calls a couple of weeks ago, one after the other: first Sotheby's, then Christie's. It had finally happened. Benny Chen had decided to cash in early, and he'd gone direct to both auction houses with a list of the pictures in his collection that he wanted to sell. And on this list were his dates of acquisition. From me. At dates well before I had apparently resold the same pictures at auction. Now the auction houses wanted me to explain what the hell was going on. If Benny Chen had bought the pictures from me, what the fuck were the versions that I had more recently resold at auction as my own property?

'I didn't return the calls of either Sotheby's or Christie's for a while because I was doing some thinking of my own. I thought, put yourself in the position of the auction houses. There are these pictures they've sold to me as the originals, then sold again as the originals – consigned by me - a couple of years later. And now here are the identical pictures also claiming to be the originals, the ones I bought from them but then sold on to Benny Chen. By now maybe someone from the auction houses will have been to see Benny Chen's versions, and realised that they're indistinguishable from the originals.'

'So their lawyers are coming after you, are they?'

'I guess so. Unless…'

'Unless what?'

'Unless they've been thinking it all out a bit further. I mean there's another reason why the international auction houses in their role as the upholders of the international art market might not want to open up this whole can of worms very much wider.'

'What's that?'

'It wouldn't be in their interests to admit that the technology exists to make perfect replicas of modern pictures. What would that do to confidence in the market? Who could be sure that the picture they owned didn't also exist in a perfect replica somewhere else? Or more to the point who could be sure that theirs wasn't the perfect replica, and the original was actually hanging on someone else's wall? What would that do to prices?'

'Wait a minute,' I said. 'Are you saying the auction houses might prefer just to suppress the whole thing rather than come after you?'

'Or to suppress the whole thing by coming after me in a more drastic way.'

'What do you mean, drastic?'

'OK then. Terminal.'

'Oh, please. Sotheby's and Christie's aren't the Mafia.'

'That's kind of what I told myself. Until this afternoon.'

'What happened this afternoon?'

'The reason I'm in Singapore now is that I thought I'd better go and chat with Mr Ho. I figured it was probably time to cut loose from him, sever our agreement, in view of the direction developments were taking. For his own protection, and mine. So that's where I went this afternoon. Guess what I found?'

'What?'

'I found his studio had been razed to the ground. In fact bits of it were still smouldering. I found Mrs Ho in tears. There'd been some kind of explosion, and then the fire that followed had been very fierce and Ho hadn't been able to get out. He'd perished with his technology. There was nothing left. I had a thousand dollars in notes in my pocket. I gave them to her. I may be a physical coward, but I hope I'm not a moral one.' He smiled briefly. It still didn't sound quite right.

'So what's it to be? The Maldives?' I asked him as I finally said goodnight and headed for my room.

'Perhaps,' he said. 'I like the sun.'

I don't think he ever got there. As I was leaving for the airport the next morning, I noticed an ambulance and a police car drawn up discreetly at a side entrance to the hotel. The hall porter, encouraged by the generous tip I had just put into his hand and the excitement of proximity to melodrama, let slip as he helped me into my taxi that there'd been a suicide last night. A guest had shot himself. I didn't ask who the guest was. Anyway, I didn't even know the name of the guy I'd been drinking whisky with into the small hours. Or whether he was a moral or a physical coward. Or both. Or neither.

Or whether indeed it was actually suicide.

Because a couple of months later I read about another fire. It was in a high-security vault in New Jersey where the international auction houses sometimes stored valuable works of art before they put them up for sale. Apparently, a collection of modern paintings belonging to a rich Chinese from Shanghai had gone up in smoke. Total write-off, a terrible accident. Two Picassos, a Chagall and a Fontana. The insurance had paid out and the man from Shanghai, name of Benny Cheng, had been fully compensated. Accidents will happen.

# Deadline

Today is Monday 5 September. I am going to keep a diary of this coming week. I think it will make it easier to come to terms with the whole thing if I write it down, observe its progress. That way I can make sense of what I'm going through, maybe even take some of the sting out of it. And perhaps it will be of interest to my great-great grandchildren. They can read it as a document of how life was lived in their ancestors' day. Who knows? By then society may have changed again, and my journal will be a bit of a curiosity, testimony of what happened to people in a different, more draconian age.

In seven days' time, on Monday 12 September, I celebrate my T-Day. Is celebrate the right word? The authorities always use it, but then it's in their interests to give the whole business a positive spin. And you can't argue with the logic, really: if something's proven to be good for society, it's right to promote it. To sugar-coat it, even. So yes, I will do my best to make my T-Day a cause for celebration. I remind myself that I voted for it when it was first introduced, a quarter of a century ago. It seemed the right thing to do. I was in my fifties then, of course, and it didn't pose an imminent problem for me personally. But now it's almost upon me, I still believe it's a good idea.

I checked the T-Day website this morning, to see if there is anything I should have done that I've missed. It starts with a sequence of calming music and images of sunlit fields and lakes and mountains. It's all very restful and relaxing, as one ever more lovely landscape follows another; and then gradually the light mellows, shadows lengthen, and the sun starts to set. It's all very cleverly done. Next they show a clip of the then Prime Minister, 25 years ago when T-Days first became law, holding forth about the glorious new era of peace and plenty that they were to usher in. 'The benefits of the system far outweigh its drawbacks,' he said. 'There may be an undertow of sentimental resistance to the new arrangements, but that will soon dissipate. The advantages to the public exchequer, to social and economic planning, to the Health Service, to pension provision, to actuarial efficiency are all too obvious to need repeating. I am convinced that this bold and revolutionary measure will appreciably increase the sum of human happiness. Everyone will be richer, spiritually and financially.'

Well of course it was a radical idea then, and it still takes some getting your head around. No-one lives beyond 82. Everyone's sojourn on this earth is gently but firmly brought to a close on their 82nd birthday. And yes, the T in T-day stands for Termination. It's all done by the state, and you plan accordingly. What is important is that there are no exemptions, not even for monarchs or prime ministers. The effect is a streamlined, totally efficient society. And it does indeed make everyone richer financially. Children know, to the day, when they're going to inherit. Pension providers know, to the day, the cut-off point of their paying out. Care homes and hospitals are not obstructed by an immobile block of the very elderly clogging up their beds. And there are no excuses for evading your T-Day. It's very rare for anyone to try to. If it happens there is certainly no publicity given to the case. The undertow of sentimental resistance did soon dissipate. In so far as it still exists, there's a very efficient branch of the police force exclusively charged with the rigorous enforcement of this particular law. No exceptions. That's the only way it can work. So we are all encouraged not just to celebrate but also to embrace our T-Day. Embrace. That's another word the authorities use a lot. It makes me feel slightly queasy: agreeing to meet the Grim Reaper is one thing, but entering into physical relations with him? I think not.

From an administrative point of view my own arrangements seem to be in order. I'm a well-organized kind of person, always have been. On the day itself I've opted for the home service. I don't like the look of those centres where you can go to have it done. Passing-on suites, they're called. They do the rooms up very nicely with flowers and so on, but it's a bit impersonal, isn't it? And what particularly horrifies me is the piped background music they apparently play throughout the building, 24 hours a day. No, not for me. I think it's less trouble all round to stay at home. You're more at ease doing it in familiar surroundings. I like the idea of doing it in the evening, too, after a drink or two. They send a team round to you. I know it's a bit more expensive, that mid-evening slot, because it's a popular time. But I think it's one of those things it's worth paying extra for. I'm due for my pre-med around 9pm. Maybe a couple of vodka and tonics in the hour before. They don't recommend more than three, do they? And that's probably the last thing I'll remember. Drifting off, after that. Gently drifting off.

Part of the celebration of T-Day is the licence you're given to make the most of the week before your 82nd birthday. It's become a tradition that you use these last seven days to do something you've always wanted to do, or to repeat an experience that's given you particular pleasure. Some go to Las Vegas for a few days, others to Venice. Some stay at home and drink heavily. Some start smoking again. Some take drugs. Some play an inordinate amount of golf. A few go on religious retreats. One lady I know spent her last day at a health spa, having her nails and hair done. She enjoyed every minute.

And what am I going to do? How am I to go out with a bang? With the help of my children, I've arranged a sequence of treats. Several slap-up meals in my favourite restaurants. There'll be no holding back on the French fries. Calories and cholesterol won't count any more by that stage. And there'll be plenty to drink, too, though with moderation. It would be a pity to waste one of your last mornings on this earth fighting a hangover. I'll be viewing several of my favourite films and rereading a couple of favourite books. Revisiting one or two of my favourite places, too, provided I can get there and back in a day. I don't want to waste too much time and effort on the hassles of travelling. There's a pleasure in just taking it easy. I might even smoke a cigarette or two. Who's counting? And then I'll be listening to music, there'll be lots of that. What would my life have been without music? Music has always been the unraveller of my knotted soul.

## Tuesday 6 September

I'm curious about something they have on offer on the T-Day website called the Happy Ending service. In the week leading up to T-Day, they send you round a nurse, of either gender depending on your preference and orientation. He or she is trained to deliver one final session of sexual pleasure, tailored to your own particular degree of physical mobility and remaining erotic capacity. There's an interview with one of them, a lady called Fiona. She's 42, and not at all a bad looker. She talks about how fulfilling her work is. I hadn't realised that it's actually a branch of the NHS. Of course they've got so much time on their hands now without all those old people to look after. It means that they can branch out into all sorts of well-being ventures. But no, this one's not for me. I don't want to be wafted to heaven on a cloud of embarrassment. I am English, after all.

Still, taking leave of my nearest and dearest is a big thing that needs careful arrangement. Two children; four grandchildren; a son-in-law and a daughter-in-law. No, they are not going to be hanging around with me on my T-Day. I've forbidden it. They will come to see me, one or two at a time in the days before. Just to make their farewells, gently, calmly, lovingly. Maybe there'll be a tear or two shed, but no hysterics. Actually, the website offers a few tips about how to part from your loved ones. Say goodbye to them, it advises, like you would if you were setting out on a journey to the other side of the world, flying to Australia perhaps. OK, in this instance you're not coming back. They'll miss you. But they'll all be considerably richer for your departure. And everything has its season, its natural span. Think of all those poor people who died before they were 82, who died unpredictably, inconveniently, maladroitly, without being able to make suitable preparation and provision or take proper farewells. They're the unlucky ones. They're the ones who cause their relations the most grief.

I won't deny that, when Patricia went early, it was tough. My dear wife was only 77. I was 79, so I've had three years without her. I could have opted for an early T-Day myself – it's something that's open to those who lose their partners before time, although there's a lot of extra paperwork – but in the end I didn't. Not out of disrespect to her. In fact she told me not to, was quite firm about it, too. 'I'll wait for you the other side,' she said. 'No point in cutting things short here when you've still a fit man and you've got your rowing and your jogging to enjoy. And your music, of course.'

'I'm sure there's music on the other side, too,' I said.

'We'll find out together,' she said, 'when you join me later.'

And it's given me three further years with my children. And grandchildren. A kind of coda, if you will, to use a musical analogy.

Do I really think now, three years on from losing Patricia, that there's any sort of life after death? Will there be music on the other side? Of course, everyone speculates privately, particularly as their own personal T-Day approaches. The introduction of T-Day has predictably strengthened the hold of organized religion on the population. Church attendance amongst those in their late seventies and early eighties markedly increased over the past quarter of a century. I have never been the most regular churchgoer myself, but I have been thinking more of these things latterly, of course I have. There used to be a thing in cricket on television called 'Win-Viz'. It calculated at any given moment in the progress of the game what the result would be, as a percentage likelihood. Team A to win, 35%. Team B, 25%. Draw 40%. As things stand now, I would calculate the possibilities of what's awaiting me as follows: Eternal Bliss 5%, some sort of Life after Death 10%, and Oblivion 85%.

Whatever the eternal Win-Viz says, I would like to have a church funeral and I've put in place requests for certain music and readings. But one thing I won't be doing is attending my own ceremony. Some people hold their funerals the day before their T-Day, but for the person who's shortly to shuffle off this mortal coil actually to be present in the church at his own obsequies is not ideal, in my experience. Those being prematurely mourned find it very difficult to adopt an appropriate manner. There's only so much benign grinning in happy reminiscence that a human being can conjure up over forty-five minutes. The result is they look either smug or desperate. And the mourners also find the process problematic. Venerating a coffin is a nice impersonal operation, indeed has a certain dignity. But venerating a live human being who's in a pew at the front and at any given moment may be scratching themselves or blowing their nose or excavating their ears for excess wax is a less satisfactory experience. Also eulogies that are delivered in the presence of the eulogee, particularly if that eulogee is fractious and opinionated, can be awkward. Facts are sometimes challenged and dates disputed. 'Oh get it right, for God's sake. How many times do I have to tell you that I was appointed vice chairman in '33, not '34.'

Joelle comes to see me today, as the youngest of the grandchildren. She comes with her mother, my daughter-in-law Laura. She's only seven, and such a pretty little girl. I keep things upbeat. I play a game of Chinese Chequers with her, which I let her win. At the end I kiss both of them, and see them off from the front door.

'Don't come out, Pop,' says Laura. 'There's a bit of a cold wind today.'

I stay where I am and wave. What am I saving myself from the cold wind for, I wonder? But I let it pass. Old habits of concern die hard. As I watch them getting into the car I just catch Joelle saying, 'Can I have an ice cream now, Mummy? You promised.'

I come back in and listen to some Bach.

## Wednesday 7 September

I go to the Oval today. With George, like we used to. And Marcus comes too, so there are three generations of us watching the cricket. My son and my grandson are at first unnaturally voluble, but gradually calm down into a companionable taciturnity, the silence broken only by the occasional statistical comment or humorous observation prompted by a misfield or an inept stroke. The tempo just as I like it. We have a good lunch in the pavilion. George has brought a bottle of champagne which makes a happy accompaniment to the afternoon session. At 2.45 I look at the scoreboard and see that Surrey are 160-3. This is perfection, I think. 160-3: it's a numerical combination that has always given me pleasure, because I believe that if the batting side lands on it a large innings total is prefigured, 350 or 400 at least. Cricket is a game that has furnished me with a rich store of statistical superstitions. And lo and behold, as the day's play approaches its end, Surrey are on a very satisfactory 372-5. We leave, by family tradition, three overs before stumps in order to avoid the rush. But, since there are only about five hundred other people in the ground, it is a superfluous precaution.

This evening, back home on my own, I pour myself a whisky and watch that old film *Casablanca*. What a load of sentimental tosh. Then that song, *A Kiss is just a Kiss*, which always made Patricia cry. For a moment I feel myself melting. Stupid, really. I pull myself together and remember to put the washing-up machine on before I go to bed.

## Thursday 8 September

Lucy was going to drive me to Sussex today, for a walk on the Downs. But it is raining hard and suddenly the prospect does not enchant. Lucy reminds me of that quotation from Marvell which says do not 'for parting pleasure strain', and so we have a lovely lunch in the local Italian trattoria instead. My daughter is very good company. And still very beautiful. Am I biased? Of course, but to look at her it's hard to believe that she has a son of 25. Which reminds me that Gerald is coming to see me on Sunday. Ah, Gerald.

To round the day off I play the entire Beethoven *Missa Solemnis*. I go to bed marvelling at its beauty, reeling under its storming of my emotions.

## Friday 9 September

Rachel comes to tea today. Well, of course teenagers are difficult, and my older granddaughter is no exception. I wouldn't want to be 16 again, I really wouldn't. If I was offered another year of life on the condition it was to be lived as a 16 year old, I'd turn it down flat. I can see she is preoccupied, awkward, a bit distant. She keeps picking up her mobile, surreptitiously glancing at it, then putting it away in her bag. 'Do look at it, darling, if you want,' I say to her. 'I really don't mind.' She turns her eyes away from me, then says no, she doesn't need to, it isn't urgent. But a couple of moments later she flicks it on, peers at it, and bursts into tears. 'I'm so sorry,' I say. 'A bit of bad news?' 'No,' she sniffles. 'It's you, Pop. I wish you didn't have to go.' I put my arm round her and we both have a bit of a cry.

## Saturday 10 September

The van from the Charity Shop comes this morning and takes away all my old suits, the ones that are still wearable that is. The rest are going to the tip in black plastic waste bags, along with my old underwear, socks, pyjamas, shirts etc. Ditto, all my shoes. I have left my books for my children to apportion between them. But I don't want to inflict on them the miserable business of sorting out a dead man's clothes. Too personal, too poignant, too squalid.

## Sunday 11 September

Gerald comes for a drink this evening, on his own. I wanted it that way, because he is my favourite grandchild. There, I've said it. Perhaps tomorrow I'll go back over this and delete it. But if I forget to, and if you ever read this, Rachel, Marcus, and Joelle, please don't be upset. I love you all equally. It's just that the first grandchild is always a bit special. And then there's been his music. He's the only one of my descendants who has shown aptitude for it. And what aptitude. I've watched his career developing with immense pride and pleasure.

'Pop, I've got a bit of good news for you,' Gerald says just before he leaves. 'I wasn't sure whether to tell you, because it's happening on Tuesday, and Tuesday is…'

'The day after T-Day,' I say. 'Don't worry. Tell me what the good news is.'

'Edgar Vaughan's gone down with appendicitis and I'm conducting in his place.'

'At The Proms?'

'At The Proms.'

'My dear fellow, that's incredible.' He's only 25, my eldest grandson. A very tender age to be making his conducting debut at the Royal Albert Hall. 'It's the most marvellous passing-on present anyone could have given me,' I say, and I mean it. 'I can't remember what's on the programme for Tuesday?'

'Mahler's Fifth.'

I embrace him. 'Thank you,' I say. 'Thank you for telling me.'

## Monday 12 September

Oh, Christ. It's not panning out as it should.

I wake up this morning still euphoric about Gerald's news. Could anything have been calculated to give me greater pleasure? Gerald conducting in the Albert Hall. Tomorrow evening. Barely twenty-four hours after my T-Day appointment tonight.

And then, as the day progresses, everything starts destabilising. I am afflicted with gathering waves of regret and resentment. And anger. Why should I miss Gerald's debut at The Proms? Why should I be compelled to forego an experience that would constitute the crowning glory of my time on this earth, to miss it by a single day? It would be a travesty if I am not there. An obscenity. I rail at the injustice, begin to construct bargains with fate, with God, with the civil authorities. If I can just be allowed to witness Gerald on that rostrum, I promise to go the moment it's over. I'll pass on, as arranged, but do it twenty-four hours later. I just need that leeway. Surely that's not too much to ask.

George and Lucy come at 6.30 this evening, as arranged, for their final farewell. Just the two of them. I don't say anything to them about my agony at missing Gerald at the Proms. It would only upset them. They don't say anything about it for the same reason, I suppose, for fear of upsetting me. But they must be proud, particularly Lucy. We hug, and my son and my daughter leave half an hour ago.

Now here I am sitting at the kitchen table with a vodka and tonic in my hand, awaiting the arrival of the T-Day team. And a crazy optimism has descended upon me. I have a knapsack standing by the kitchen door. It contains two cheese sandwiches, an apple, and a bottle of water. It's a simple enough plan. I'm going to spend the night in Hyde Park, holed up in the bushes. I've chosen Hyde Park because of its proximity to the Albert Hall, for obvious reasons. The question is how to survive till tomorrow evening, once I'm a non-person. My identity will be cancelled automatically at 9 p.m. this evening. From then on I can't use a bank card, a passport, a driving licence, or a mobile. I can't buy food or drink, take a train or a plane, a bus or a taxi, or drive a car. I don't know how quickly they come after you once you're reported as being on the run. I've heard they can track you down pretty much anywhere, because they don't switch off your location bleeper implant until they have what they call 'proof of demise'. If I want to give myself a better chance of temporary survival I need somehow to switch that location bleeper off. It's a chip implanted in my left shoulder. Am I brave enough to dig it out with a penknife to disable it? I am confident I could bear the pain, but I don't want to botch the job and bleed to death.

Perhaps with a bit of luck they won't come after me till tomorrow. Then I'll try and get through the day in as close proximity to as many other people as possible, commuters, tourists, crowds of shoppers, anything to make it more difficult for them to pin me down. And there's the question of access to the Albert Hall. I haven't got a ticket, of course. I could see what's doing at the box office, but that's going to be difficult without a bank card. I could try and sneak in with the Promenaders. Or pose as a member of the orchestra. I'll find a way. I feel an extraordinary elation at the challenge of it all. Ridiculous, I know, but I am struck by a sense of destiny too.

The T-day team have just arrived. They are a friendly crew, led by a jolly woman who tells me her name is Gwyneth. She has two assistants, Fred and Nobby. I have instructed them to set up in my bedroom while I go to the kitchen to pour myself another vodka and tonic. 'You do that, my lovey,' calls Gwyneth. 'I'd have one with you if I wasn't on duty.' Very shortly now I shall nip out of the back door with my knapsack and take to my bicycle.

*It was Gwyneth's shout in the pub that night, after they'd finished the last job of their evening shift. They sat down with their drinks, and she sighed philosophically.*

*'You can almost smell it, can't you,' she said, 'with the ones that are planning to do a bunk. I could tell this last one was a runner, something about the look in his eyes.'*

*'The bicycle at the garden gate with the rolled-up sleeping bag on the back was a bit of a give-away, too,' said Fred.*

*'Well, at least he didn't put up too much of a fight,' said Nobby.*

*'And it's wonderful to watch them calming down once they've had the happy jab, isn't it?' continued Gwyneth. 'Though if I'd been*

*him I wouldn't have chosen to go out to all that gloomy music. I asked him who was the composer. Fellow called Mahler, he said. Enough to make you want to top yourself.'*

# Basil In Basel

Not many people have heard of the writer Basil Colligy. He died young, and as far as I am aware only published one novel. I came across it by chance, when randomly grazing the London Library stacks. I like that word grazing. It was first coined by Thomas Carlyle, who talked about the pastures that the London Library offers to serious literary ruminants such as myself, people who have the leisure to nose about its expanses in search of seren-dipitous literary cud to chew. There are more than a million books on open shelves. They line a labyrinth of passages and halls and basements on a perplexity of different levels. You can easily get lost. It's rumoured that some evenings search parties are sent out to rescue disorientated readers who are still wander-ing blindly down indistinguishable metal alleyways. I was scan-ning a shadowy corner of Fiction CAR-COU when I found *The Guilty Bicycle*. It had been published in 1938. I noted from the date stamps on the library label at the front of the book that it had only been taken out six times in its life, the latest in 1991. It had slumbered untouched for the last thirty years.

I was expecting *The Guilty Bicycle* to be a detective story, indeed was looking forward to it because the 1930s were a golden age for the genre. But no, it was something rather different, an odd blend of surrealism and science fiction with tinges of Saki and Alfred Jarry. The protagonist is a philosopher-cyclist called Bernard who, in between speeding around the country thwarting a conspiracy to abolish the colour yellow, invents a robot that he programmes to spout forth a stream of Confucian aphorisms.

The first one that the robot comes up with is hard to interpret: *The convalescent has no memory of snow.* It is followed by the scarcely less opaque *Cathedrals make bad hospitals*, and *Do not offer pomegranates to a sleeping tiger.* But gradually, by dint of rewiring and fine tuning, Bernard renders his robot (whom he christens Eric) more coherent, capable of utterances of increasing intelligibility. Soon Eric is warning that *Behind sunlit doors lie dark passages,* vouchsafing that *No man should prune his own bamboo* and then, showing a certain literary awareness, asserting *Better legless in Babylon than eyeless in Gaza.* Bernard is on the whole pleased with his mechanical *protégé*'s progress.

Then one night at 2.30 am Eric has such a surge of insightful creativity that he overheats his mechanism and nearly blows a gasket. He bellies forth in quick succession *Small trees cast long shadows, Who lies in the long grass dies of the snake bite, The deaf man follows the brightest peacock,* and *One bicycle is worth three elephants.* Bernard is anxious that Eric should not overstrain himself, so he switches him off for a few hours. Upon reactivation the next afternoon, Eric proclaims authoritatively *Better a strong ox than a beautiful woman.*

This one gives Bernard - who has romantic inclinations - some pause for thought, so he challenges Eric on it. After a lot of bad-tempered clanking an alternative spews forth: *Better a beautiful ox than a strong woman.* His chivalry aroused, Bernard presses for a further revision and finally elicits from the curmudgeonly Eric *Better a strong woman than a beautiful ox.* It is a compromise which leaves neither master nor machine entirely satisfied.

Eric is still prone to temperamental days when he becomes deliberately obscure. On one particularly difficult morning he pronounces *Better the drone of the fly than the desire of the mosquito, Seek not irony in a she-elephant,* and *You cannot find Belief without first strangling a few wart-hogs.*

At this point Bernard has to cycle off to a colourist convention in Welwyn Garden City where he delivers an impassioned defence of yellowism. A detachment of Redists attempt to kidnap him, but he eludes them and returns home to tinker further with Eric's mechanism, tightening a couple of bolts. As a result Eric starts to grapple with weightier questions, averring that *The death of an artist is not always a tragedy,* and *Dead war heroes make poor fathers.* Bernard finds some engine oil and feeds it to Eric, which precipitates an exhortation to *Seek perpetual blossom not in the orchard but in the opium pipe,* and a warning that *The whitest washing does not come from the most honourable laundries.*

Bernard finally wins his heroic battle to save the power of yellow. But in the last chapter of the book Eric's tone becomes more ominous: *Beware the hairdresser with blunt scissors,* he counsels; and *Avoid the one-armed dentist.* Indeed the very last page of the novel consists of a single sentence – presumably a final contribution from Eric - printed in unexpectedly large type:

*Do not walk beneath the upstairs window of the owner of heavy books*

I couldn't get this last piece of wisdom out of my head. Eric was apparently warning against the danger of death or serious injury by falling weighty tome. I am rather a connoisseur of strange hurtlings to earth in fiction: a character in a Graham Greene short story who is killed by a pig falling from the balcony of a tenement in Naples; frozen urine ejected from an airliner in a solid block that crashes through the roof of a house belonging to someone in a David Lodge novel; a dead dog – again ejected from an aircraft - landing on a roof where a man and woman are sunbathing in Huxley's *Eyeless in Gaza*; a Father Brown story in which a crazed cleric throws a hammer from the top of his church tower on to the head of an unrepentant sinner below. Was this potentially another example to add to my list?

I was curious about the author. His biography as supplied in the book itself (published by an imprint called the Grenadine Press) was brief and told me the following:

*Basil Colligy is a writer and journalist. He was born in 1908 and was brought up in the West Country of England. He has travelled widely in recent years, living variously in Toulon, Zurich, Gibraltar, Cairo and Tangier. The Guilty Bicycle is his first novel.*

But my further research into Colligy didn't turn up much else. I thought I had found a reference to him in the diaries of Robert Bruce Lockhart, but it proved to be a different Basil.

I looked for his name in vain in the correspondence of the Surrealists. I turned my attention to the Grenadine Press, but that led nowhere. They flourished briefly in the 1930s and were never heard of again. Had Colligy written other novels? There was nothing further by him in the London Library. Extensive trawling on the internet produced very little. Colligy was apparently a one-book wonder. He had probably died in the war, I concluded. He was of that generation.

In due course I returned *The Guilty Bicycle* to the London Library, thwarted. But Colligy stayed with me, niggled at me. I decided at least to acquire my own copy of the book as a homage to its mysterious creator. But even with the aid of Abe Books and Amazon I couldn't find one. There was not a single copy of *The Guilty Bicycle* for sale anywhere in the second-hand book market of the world. Was it possible that a book published considerably less than a century ago could vanish off the face of the earth? Perhaps. Say the original print run was no more than a few hundred copies. Say sales were sluggish. Say what remained unsold with the publishers was finally pulped. That would leave a couple of hundred in contemporary circulation, comprising those sold, sent for review, or given away by the proud author to more or less eager recipients. Over a couple of generations that number could diminish to almost zero with dilapidations, house clearances, mislayings on trains, receding levels of interest in the author. It suddenly seemed a sad fate for a work of such originality. And it made me even more determined to learn more about Colligy.

There was one more potential lead that I had noted but not yet investigated, the printed dedication at the beginning of the book, which read as if it had emanated out of Eric. '*To Orla Jeavons. Better the fragrance of a lemon tree than the crispness of a banknote.*' Who was Orla Jeavons? With the help of the internet you can track down almost anyone these days. Within a week I was in email contact with Magda Fenchurch. She was Orla Jeavons's granddaughter, and she lived in Oxford. She told me that her grandmother had died in 1991. It was interesting that I was asking about Basil Colligy because she'd recently been going through some old letters that she'd inherited from her grandmother, and there were a few from someone of that name. Would I like to see them? I arranged to come to her house for tea.

I supposed she was an academic, or a schoolteacher. She was rather attractive, in a gaunt, severe way. Perhaps she had inherited these vestigial good looks from her grandmother.

'I hadn't realised Mr Colligy was a novelist,' she said. 'Did he write much?'

'Only one book as far as I know. And he dedicated it to your grandmother.'

'I realised he must have been a bit of a beau of hers. From the correspondence.'

'But you haven't read the book?'

'No. Well, I suppose he must have given her a copy, as he dedicated it to her. But it hasn't survived. And of course he died in the war.'

'Killed in action?'

She looked at me oddly, as if I had made a joke in poor taste. 'In a manner of speaking. But have a look at the letters, they'll give it to you from the horse's mouth.'

There were only three. She handed them to me in date sequence, one by one.

*Tangier, 5 March 1939*

*Sweetest angel,*

*I spend my days here lotus-eating. Why don't you join me? Life is really very pleasant. Drink is copious and cheap. Ditto, servants. There is no shortage of urchins in the street outside eager to sell me their sisters. Or brothers, depending on my taste. I sit on my roof and watch the sunset, opening another bottle and thinking irenic thoughts. All I am really lacking is you.*

*Do you remember that evening when I punted us up the Cherwell by moonlight and you lay in my arms as we listened to the nightingales? Neither do I, but I wish we had.*

*I know there are many, but I claim without doubt to be your sincerest and most ardent admirer,*
*B.*

*Gibraltar, 6 September 1941*

*My beautiful one,*

*If I consigned this letter to what passes for the international postal system in these unusual times, it would certainly never reach you. To avoid it becoming the plaything of voyeurs and censors and espionage agents I am entrusting it to a friend called Edward who is setting off for London via Lisbon today. He is a deeply reliable fellow and he will deliver it to you by hand.*

*Things have become rather colourful here. I am having to cultivate acquaintance with some remarkably unsavoury characters. But you once observed that I have a penchant for the gutter, so perhaps I am merely gravitating to my natural habitat. I pass often between Tangier and Gibraltar, and it is probable that I will be on the move further afield in the coming weeks. I have something to deliver, which will mean making my way up to Lisbon and taking an aeroplane flight to Switzerland. If by some unlikely chance you felt moved to write to me, you could give the letter to Edward when you see him, as he and I will meet up again in Basel in a couple of months. But of course you may be too busy to write because I know your contribution to the war effort involves regular attendance at a wide variety of London night clubs in your selfless mission to keep up the morale of as many of our fighting men as possible. Seriously, my sweet, please be careful of yourself. I am very, very attached to you. I don't like the idea of bombs falling on you.*

*Very much love,*

*B.*

The last one that she handed me was not from Colligy:

*Basel, 12 November 1941*

*Dear Miss Jeavons,*

*I promised Basil that if anything ever happened to him I would let you know, and it is now my sad duty to write to tell you that Basil was killed on Friday. It was a tragic accident, here in Basel where he had arrived last week.*

*Basil was walking down Bahnhofstrasse when an object — a heavy book, I understand - fell from a top floor window and hit him on the head. He died instantly. It was an incredibly unlucky chance. But although I can't go into details, I hope it will be some consolation to you that he gave his life in the service of his country.*

*I know how deeply he felt about you. Please accept my pro-foundest sympathies for your loss.*

*Yours sincerely,*

*Edward Mayhew*

I drove home rather thoughtfully.

# Natalia

The Mayfair restaurant where Hugo Conrad invited Natalia Manasseh to lunch was punitively expensive, the audacity of its prices being matched only by the meagreness of its portions. As they were shown to their table Hugo thought two things: first, he was very glad that Rokeby's were picking up the bill; and second that Natalia was probably the most glamorous, exotic and gorgeous woman he had ever eaten lunch with. He was so nervous that his own voice sounded strained and unfamiliar when he first addressed words to her. But he ordered a bottle of Sancerre and gradually he relaxed. He found she was easy to talk to. He began to dream impossible dreams.

'Tell me about your childhood,' he said, reaching into that section of his extensive conversational repertoire marked Establishing Intimacy. 'Where were you brought up?'

She put down her wine glass and touched the corner of her lips with her napkin. 'This you do not need to know, my friend,' she said. 'This is empty quarter.'

Perhaps she genuinely couldn't remember any longer. Perhaps she didn't choose to. Either way, Natalia's origins had been wiped from the record. They were no longer relevant to her life, to what she did now. It was as if she had been born fully-formed on the autumn day in 1995 when she arrived in St Petersburg, at the railway station, aged seventeen. She had travelled twenty-one hours in a train with a girlfriend called Olga from a tiny village in the Urals to get work in the big city. Or at least Olga had come to get work. But Natalia had come to make her fortune.

Olga went back to the village in the Urals after ten days, defeated, but Natalia was determined. Natalia stayed on. She found a job in a cafe which came with a tiny room above the premises, a room barely bigger than a cupboard, in which Yuri the cafe owner allowed her to sleep. The important thing about the room was it had a lock. Thus she could repel the occasional late night advances of the drunken Yuri beating on her door. Such attempted intrusions were an occupational hazard. She was already adept at looking after herself.

With what she saved from her first month's wages she bought one very beautiful and expensive dress. She made the investment because she reasoned to herself that you could not wear more than one dress at a time. The people who saw her in this very beautiful dress were not to know it was the only thing in her wardrobe. When she wore it she was just as good as the richest women in St Petersburg. Better, actually, because she was more beautiful than most of them.

On the one evening a week when she was not obliged to work in the cafe she would slide into her one very beautiful, very expensive dress, cover herself in a nondescript overcoat, and make her way to the bar in the Grand Hotel where the rich foreign businessmen stayed. Once she removed her overcoat, it was like a butterfly emerging from a chrysalis. She found that many of the rich foreign businessmen were eager to buy her drinks. She wasn't stupid. She knew what they wanted from her; but she also knew how to get what she wanted from them. It was money, of course, and she made plenty of that; but it was also an education, a key to how the rich did things. She learned quickly, learned how to present herself, learned how to talk to men. Quite soon she had done well enough to give up her job at the cafe. She found she had enough money to rent her own small apartment. A studio flat, just off Nevsky Prospect. She preferred to live on her own, with the one person in the world she knew she could trust.

She was determined. And she learned the benefits of commercial intransigence. It was an extension of the principle she had grasped instinctively the first night she found herself, aged seventeen, in a bedroom of the Grand Hotel alone with a man. Money first, she told him. Five hundred dollars. Cash. In my hand. Now. Otherwise I walk out of here. No-one had told her this was how you transacted. It came naturally to her, even then.

She went on learning. One of the things that she learned was to give the sort of men that she met in the bars of the Grand Hotel and the Astoria a little bit of melodrama, to construct a romantic back-story to herself. Natalia's back-story was that she was an impecunious music student. It was a creation of her own imagination but one that went down well, a lot better than telling the men she met that she had recently arrived in Peter after a twenty-one hour train journey from oblivion.

'By day, I study at music conservatory,' she would inform her enrapt companion over champagne in the low light of the hotel bar. 'By night I am here. This work I must do in order to pay my conservatory fees.' Sometimes, to give the story an extra flourish, she would draw two parallel lines on the table in front of them. 'See, top line is my life at music conservatory. Bottom line is my life at night. If two lines are crossing, personal catastrophe.'

Her companion would nod, concerned, enchanted. 'What instrument do you play?'

Generally she said the piano, occasionally the violin. Now and then she embroidered the myth with the cello. There was something erotic about the size of the cello, the idea of her own long and shapely physical undulations entwining about a musical instrument with its own rich and generous curves. The punters loved it. She gave them what they wanted. She was a quick learner.

'I would love to hear you play...' the inebriated investment banker from Frankfurt or the entranced corporate lawyer from London would murmur sentimentally, moving his chair closer to hers.

'One day, perhaps. If we know each other better.'

There were certain realities you had to observe as a lady of the night. In order to operate as successfully as she did in and around the top hotels and night clubs of the city, she needed protection. She chose a thug called Arkady as her protector because he was the most powerful of the pimps and, in exchange for thirty per cent of her earnings she could rely on the security that he and his boys provided. She was good at judging who to rely on, even when it came to pimps. Particularly when it came to pimps.

Her increasing success in the top hotels of St Petersburg enabled her to do certain things that she'd always wanted to do. One was to increase her wardrobe. She did not buy many clothes, but she continued to buy the best. Whenever she went out in the evenings, she looked stunning. And very much classier than most of her competitors. The other thing that her success gave her was free time in the mornings and afternoons. This she put to good use. The same instinct that told her men liked to imagine her as a music student now persuaded her to broaden her cultural repertoire to include the visual arts. She had once on a whim dropped into the Hermitage Museum, curious as to what she would find behind the imposing facade beside the Neva that she'd often walked by. She was immediately fascinated by what she saw, and she took to spending many hours looking at the art. She learned about Rembrandt; she learned about Boucher and Hubert Robert; she learned about Picasso and Matisse; and she learned about Shchukin and Morozov, the extraordinary Russian collectors of the last days of the Tsarist regime, without whom there would be no great works by Matisse and Picasso for her to admire in the Hermitage now.

So the conversation with which she enchanted visiting Swedish industrialists and London venture capitalists now broadened to include paintings and painters as well. 'One day I would like to own a Matisse,' she confided to an Italian civil engineer.

'A woman as beautiful as you should own twenty Matisses,' the Italian assured her, staring into her eyes.

She had never heard anything so absurd in her life. Twenty Matisses. She only wanted one. But she put her hand on his arm and murmured, 'You are sweet man, Francesco, you know that?'

At a certain point she realised she had learned all the lessons that were available to her in St Petersburg. The final lesson she absorbed was that there were other, richer fields of operation for her in places like Paris and New York and London. And after two years of patrolling the bar at the Grand Hotel and the Astoria, she moved on. The first phase of her education was over.

Perhaps she had subconsciously decided that she was destined for the capitals of western Europe quite early on, from the moment she opened an account for her ever-growing savings in the St Petersburg branch of a London bank. She took a one-way ticket on a flight to London and began the second phase of her self-education. She travelled business class. She felt it would be a worthwhile investment, in the same way that her designer dresses and hours spent in the Hermitage were an investment. She found herself sitting next to an Englishman who was only too happy to draw her into conversation. The Englishman was called David and turned out to be a property developer. From his real estate portfolio he was delighted to find her a comfortable one bedroom flat in Bayswater, at a very reasonable rent. She moved into it three days later.

Sometimes, later on, people suggested that she had been lucky in the way things turned out for her. 'No,' she would correct them. 'This was not luck. This was will. If you have will, you make your own luck. I know this to be true. The things that happened to me in my life are proof of it.'

David paid many attentions to her for the first three months of her existence in London. Judiciously she encouraged them. It was convenient to be taken out to dinners, and to find her way about the city: which were the best hotels, the best restaurants, the places where you met the richest men. But she knew she was going to have to move on from David. He was a good man, but her instinct – highly tuned in such matters – told her that while he was rich, he was not rich enough. She had her sights trained on bigger game. Also he was showing signs of clinging, of wanting to see her too often. He was getting in her way. A clean cut must be made. She discovered – it was not difficult, she was a resourceful woman – that in a suburb called Esher he had a wife called Elaine and three young children, children on whom he doted. She tracked down the email address of his wife. It was sad, but she had to do it: she forwarded to Elaine – from her husband, as if in error - an intimate and highly compromising message directed to Natalia making reference to the apartment in which he had installed her and the hours of pleasure that he was sporadically allowed to enjoy with her there. The consequences were almost immediate. Shamefacedly David sent her a message two days later that there had been a complication, that she must move out of the Bayswater flat as soon as she reasonably could. That was no problem. Natalia had already identified a rather nicer place that she could now afford in Cadogan Square. To be on the safe side, she never let David know its address.

As in Russia, she gravitated to the smart hotels. These were still the places where you could meet suitable men. One evening, in the ladies' loo in Claridges, she fell into conversation with a very glamorous woman wearing a lot of jewellery.

'You are Russian?' the woman asked her.

Natalia agreed that she was.

'Me too. I am Anya.'

Natalia liked Anya immediately. She was a little older than Natalia, and clever and funny.

'You... you work round here?' Natalia asked her cautiously.

'No, no, darlink. I used to be like you, maybe, working girl. But now I am married woman, darlink. Very rich husband, a banker no less, so no need for working.'

'That's marvellous,' said Natalia in genuine admiration.

'Something more marvellous, darlink: I am soon to be ex-married woman. I am divorcing William.'

'Oh, I am sorry.'

'No need for sorry, darlink. It's the best news. You know why?'

'Why?'

'He's giving me big settlement for alimony. Also my own flat, round the corner in Lowndes Square. I insisted. Lowndes Square, William, I said. Nothing less. So now I am free and rich. Mrs Anya Wallace, at your service.'

After that Natalia and Anya became friends. They quite often met up to discuss their respective progress in London society.

'You must not make yourself too available, darlink,' Anya advised her, in the women-only beauty spa where they sometimes spent whole days together. 'Let men take you out to dinner, but not necessary to sleep with them immediately. Tease them a bit, which make them want you even more. This also makes for gifts, expensive ones. But be careful of Dukes.'

'What is Dukes?'

'Dukes, they are very big deal in British society. Top men, almost as good as royal family. Aristocrats, know what I mean. Very rich. I have been close friend with one of them. But my God, darlink, he was tight. No good expecting jewellery from Dukes. You know what he gave me for Christmas once? A complimentary British Airways toiletries bag. Can you believe it? Not even First Class, only Business.'

Natalia shook her head in shock at the revelation. But the overall strategy of how to treat men (excluding Dukes) struck her as sensible. It was pleasing to have the conclusions she had reached on her own initiative confirmed by such a patently successful practitioner as Anya. Natalia was in the process of driving a very rich Chinese called Kenny Sung almost to distraction by having dinner with him regularly but never quite yielding her full favours. Each time she saw him she managed to extort from him a yet more valuable piece of jewellery. She showed the latest piece to Anya the following week over tea after another spa session.

'Not bad,' said Anya approvingly, examining it with the eye of an expert. 'Is piece from Melmot. Must have cost £15,000.'

'Melmot?'

'Top jeweller in London. They know everything, especially Fabergé. Next time you ask Kenny Sung to give you Fabergé egg.'

Natalia nodded doubtfully. 'But Anya I have to tell you something. I am thinking I really don't want a Fabergé collection. I am thinking I would rather have the cash.'

'No problem, darlink. You come with me now, I introduce you to my friend at Melmot.'

Natalia warmed to the man at Melmot immediately. He was small and bald, and avuncular and deferential at the same time, and he was called Mr Jenkins. He was the soul of politeness and discretion. 'It is a great pleasure to see you again, Mrs Wallace,' he said to Anya. 'How is your husband?'

'Ex-husband,' said Anya. 'No, no need for condolence. All very amicable. So, I have brought very dear friend of mine to meet you, Mr Jenkins. May I present you to Madame Natalia.'

'How do you do.'

'Madame Natalia has a piece, a very beautiful piece, acquired from your good selves, that she would like to do business with you on.'

'But of course. Won't you come through to the private room?'

Natalia produced the necklace that Kenny Sung had given her. Mr Jenkins took it in his hand and nodded happily. 'Yes, yes, this came from us. No problem at all.'

'Madame Natalia would wish you to buy back, Mr Jenkins. Now let's be practical. What did you sell it for? Something around £15,000, I am guessing.'

Mr Jenkins went a little pink about the cheeks as he consulted his computer screen. 'Really, Mrs Wallace, you're a better expert than any of us. You'll be putting the entire London trade out of business if you carry on like this. You're absolutely spot on, 15,000. I do congratulate you, I really do.'

'So you buy it back now from Madame Natalia? For cash?'

'With pleasure. Particularly as she is a friend of yours.'

'How much you give, Mr Jenkins?' Anya was remorseless.

He sucked his teeth and peered again at the computer screen. 'We could probably say 6,500.'

'Nine would be more generous, Mr Jenkins.'

Mr Jenkins frowned. 'I might stretch to £7,000.'

'Madame Natalia, I am thinking, will come to you often in the future, sometimes with even better things. She can choose from which shop her admirers buy her gifts. She has many admirers, Mr Jenkins. Be generous now and she will be loyal to you. Call it 7,500 and you have a deal.'

'7,500 it is, for two such charming ladies,' said Mr Jenkins gallantly.

Mr Jenkins disappeared to lay hands on the requisite number of banknotes. 'That's about the going rate,' murmured Anya when he was out of the room. 'Fifty per cent of the cost price to buy it back in cash, darlink. Remember that for future.'

When Mr Jenkins came back in with a fat envelope in his hand, Anya seized him by the sleeve. 'And if emergency happens? Mr Jenkins, explain to Madame Natalia your emergency plan.'

'Ah. Yes. The emergency plan. Well, if a situation should arise whereby – um – the original purchaser of the piece should unexpectedly wish to see the piece about your person on a particular occasion, even though you have already returned it to us, we will make every effort to make it available to you on temporary loan for that one occasion. Provided of course it has not in the meantime been resold.'

'Once,' Anya told Natalia as they got into a taxi after the transaction, 'I was given the same earrings three times by the same man. Each time I cashed them in at Melmot and they returned them to stock, and each time he came in again and bought them for me. He had no memory, poor boy. Nothing between the ears. Too much white powder if you get my meaning.'

One day Anya told Natalia about something called targeting.

'Targeting?' Natalia asked.

'It is about thinking longer term. You must not be passive in the selection of the men you go out with. Sometimes you must be pro-active. So you find a target, a very rich one. This means research. Who are the bankers who are making the most money? These are people to meet, darlink. So, you find one. You find one very rich who goes to gym. The ones who go to gym are vain ones. This means they take care of bodies. This means they will look at your body, too. So, you find out where he goes to gym. Will be expensive, exclusive place with very big membership fee. You become member there too. No matter if it costs thousands of pounds, is money well spent. You make sure you are working out at same time as target. If necessary, you make friends with gym staff, get them to put you on machinery next to him. Then there is no problem for you. He will make conversation to you, hundred per cent. Ask you for drink. No looking back. No matter if he's married. You will be the sort of girl he'll leave his wife for. Is how I met William.'

The upper reaches of smart London society, Natalia realised, were the habitat of two distinct but interdependent species - the rich, and those who provided services to the rich. The commodity that women like Anya and Natalia were supplying, beautifully packaged and presented, was themselves.

'You are clever girl, you can talk, you know about life,' continued Anya. 'You must be always taking care to learn: to learn wine, art, music. Then – bap-bap-bap – married. Soon – bap-bap-bap – split up. Good lawyers, and you can come away five million richer. Is easy peasy.'

It was easy peasy. Natalia identified Eric Manasseh from research she had done on the internet, and in the rich-lists of various business publications and Sunday newspapers. He was the CEO of a financial institution. A big financial institution. Judicious further inquiries established that he was a member of an exclusive gym not far from the Bank of England, and that he quite often chose to work out there between 7 and 8 in the evening. Even better, he was recently divorced. One evening in February Natalia identified him exercising on a rowing machine. Casually she walked over and took up her own position on the machine next to him. She had recently treated herself to a week's holiday in the Caribbean and she knew she was looking good. She had on a white T-shirt and shorts calculated to make her legs seem very, very long. She began a slow but purposeful motion backwards and forwards, backwards and forwards. Out of the corner of her eye she saw he was resting for a moment, and that he was looking in her direction. So she brought her own sequence to a gentle conclusion, leant forward and smiled across at him.

'Why do we do it to ourselves?' she heard him asking her.

'You don't like to exercise?'

'There are things I'd rather be doing.'

'Like what?'

'Relaxing with a drink.'

'This drink you must earn,' she told him seriously. 'No pleasure without suffering.'

Twenty minutes later, when he'd finished his session, he smiled at her again. She'd noticed, out of the corner of her eye, that he had really been pushing himself. Showing off a bit. There was a generous garland of sweat round the neck of his T shirt. As he stood up a trifle wearily, draping a towel round his neck, he murmured to her, 'I think I've earned my drink.'

'Perhaps you have.'

'Won't you join me?'

It was all too easy. The following week he invited her to dinner. Natalia really turned it on, a concerted display of elegant flirtatiousness with conversation encompassing music, art, and cinema. In fact she found she knew considerably more about the arts than Eric did. Poor Eric did not stand a chance. As Natalia described it to Anya, it was textbook operation.

'Yes, darlink,' agreed Anya, 'you are quick learner. You choose well with this Eric, he make very suitable first husband.'

Initially Natalia's marriage was a happy one. Eric took her to many places. He liked to show her off. He introduced her to

222

people that he knew, powerful people in the financial world. And a few politicians. Also some actors, some entrepreneurs, even a minor member of the Royal family.

Natalia began going to art galleries in London, too. She took up where she had left off in the Hermitage. She went by day to The Royal Academy, the National Gallery, and the Tate Modern. And she discovered the international auction houses as well. She was fascinated by how much things sold for, particularly contemporary art. She even persuaded Eric to buy one or two pieces, at prices in the range of £50,000 - £100,000. 'Not expenditure, darlink,' she told him. 'Investment.'

But nothing is for ever, not like in the fairy stories. Eric was a good man, a hard-working man. But perhaps that was the problem: he worked too hard. Also, he was predictable. She knew the way his mind functioned, she always knew what he would say next. She knew the jokes that would make him laugh, the same stories he would always tell. By the end, she thought she would scream. She just wasn't built for living with the same man indefinitely. In the end men became boring. Suffocating. So, after two years' marriage to Eric, she got divorced from him. She followed Anya's prescription: 'Always amicable, darlink. Is better for both.'

Natalia had hot and implacable lawyers. In the final separation agreement from Eric she banked several million, perhaps not quite enough to secure her future, but enough to make her comfortable for a few years, and enough, more immediately, to take a long holiday. She disappeared to the Caribbean for three weeks. When she came back to London she found she had moved up a level in terms of social desirability. The fact that she had been married to Manasseh gave her an extra degree of respectability. She kept his name, and that, coupled with her natural class and style, meant that more doors were open to her. It was no longer necessary to frequent expensive gyms. Rich men pursued her, not just because they hoped to sleep with her but because they enjoyed her company. She played the field a bit, at a fairly elevated level: she was seen at dinner with one of the lesser Saudi princes.

She found she liked art more and more. She went to many exhibitions and got invited to the private views of big sales at the international auction houses. Her instinct told her that while, as she had discovered through Melmot, it was a good thing to know about jewellery and its value, even more doors were opened to you if you knew about art. She studied artists' names, and she followed prices. She noted the ones that were on the up, particularly the rising stars of the Contemporary market. For rich friends and acquaintances she occasionally found expensive pictures, on which she made increasingly substantial commissions. She reconnected with her old financial intransigence. On more than one occasion she found herself repeating the words to which she had first given utterance in the bedrooms of the smarter St Petersburg hotels: 'If you want the best, darlink, it is necessary to pay for it. My price is my price.'

The professional reason why Hugo Conrad had invited Natalia to lunch was that he wanted to show her Mrs Ortega's Picasso. Over coffee he passed across his mobile so that she could see an image of it; in view of the size of the artist's erection the action of revealing it to her simultaneously horrified and excited him. She glanced momentarily at the painting but it didn't seem to engage her.

'It's a really good example,' he persisted. 'And it's not expensive at $28 million. Do you think you might have someone for it?'

'Perhaps.' She laid his mobile face down on the white tablecloth, and looked him in the eyes. 'Listen, I want you to help me, Hugo.'

'Of course, if I can.'

'You know about rich men in London. They are clients of Rokeby's, you have records. So you do me a favour please.' She mentioned the name of someone who occupied a position of awe and reverence on the Rokeby's client data base, a man with whom Hugo had had some discreet professional dealings. 'Is this man rich? He is very successful. I think I am right, yes? So he is rich man worth many millions? Or is it billions, Hugo? I need to know.'

'Why do you need to know?'

'Because he is asking me for dinner,' she said impatiently.

He felt a little sick but said he would look into it. 'And the Picasso?' he persisted.

She moved her head slowly from side to side in a gesture of equivocation. 'We'll see.'

She called again the following morning asking Hugo if he had news for her. Hugo prevaricated, but there was an urgency in her tone. He sensed that not only was she out of his league as a lover, but also the dynamic of their professional relationship was changing. She was no longer looking to him to provide expertise about paintings, or opportunities to make profitable sales, but for information about people; more explicitly she was seeking the financial data needed to identify whom she should or should not accept as suitors. Her next husband was being lined up. It was an entirely commercial decision, and one she could make more easily with the aid of Rokeby's client database.

Rather bitterly, Hugo asked himself if he was thinking laterally enough here. Weren't the New York management encouraging staff to reach out to new clients and embrace new ways of doing business in order to broaden the company franchise? Was this an opportunity to create a new revenue stream? Perhaps, if he gave her the confidential data she requested, Rokeby's could charge her an Introductory Commission once she achieved matrimony. But calculated on the basis of what? The net worth of her new husband? Or at least the value of his art collection? Later in the day Hugo called her back and told her what he knew. The answer to her question was in the billions rather than the millions.

That evening Hugo went out and got very drunk.

The next time Hugo saw Natalia was four weeks later. It was at a private view, and she was on the arm of the man about whose wealth she had interrogated Hugo at lunch. Hugo watched them at a distance. It is always a difficult decision with the very rich how to approach them in a social context. Some like to be made much of; others are irked by the unsolicited attentions of service-providers. On this occasion Hugo went up to him to say hello. The man was urbane, charming, smooth, and spoke English with an accent that was like an autobiography. It linked both ends of the Mediterranean, originating somewhere between Aleppo and Beirut and being overlaid sometimes with the hoarse mellifluity of a Monegasque gigolo, and at others with the hectoring asperity of a ruthless Mafioso businessman. Now he was polite, perhaps even rather proud to be able to introduce Hugo to his glamorous companion.

'Do you know my fiancée, Natalia Manasseh?' Before Hugo could speak, Natalia said: 'No, we have not met. How do you do, Mr Conrad.'

But as she held out her hand, her eye gave him the quick flicker of a wink.

Milton Keynes UK
Ingram Content Group UK Ltd.
UKHW041814210923
429134UK00002B/9

9 781912 914562